Meant

QC Ngo

ISBN:

Warning

This book is for mature audiences due to its language, violence, and sexual content.

Table of Contents

Chapter 1
Unwanted

On a snowy Christmas Eve, a young Vietnamese woman placed a baby on the church's doorstep. She rang the doorbell and quickly hid behind a bush, waiting for someone to come out.

Just a few hours before that, the agonizing sound of her birthing was drowning out by carol singers at a nearby house. All alone on a cold winter day and scared, she struggled to pull the baby out of her.

As a teenager, for fear of being disowned by her parents, she has hidden her pregnancy and secretively gave birth to a baby girl in the back of a navy blue Rav4. A fearful moment that she could not have foreseen when she lay with a boy for the first time.

A little later, the door opened, and a nun stepped out. Mother Mary looked around before noticing the baby wrapped in a beige towel at her feet.

"Well, hello, there," Mother Mary said as she crouched down to pick up the baby. Dressed in black from head to toe, she has a face that lightens up the night. "What a precious little one. It must be a gift from heaven. Let's get you warm up," Mother Mary said as she headed inside.

The young woman felt relief and walked away crying, hoping that her baby would forgive her. She wondered if she would have a chance to reunite with her daughter in the future.

*****

Seven years later, his mother dropped nine-year-old Wriley Corva at a local orphanage run by the church.

"I'm sorry, Wriley. Your father never came back. I can't raise two kids on my own. Your sister is too young. I have to be with her. You're better off here with warm clothes and three meals a day," Wriley's mother said as she walked him inside.

Wriley followed his mother quietly. They went into Mother Mary's office, who welcomed Wriley with open arms.

"Thank you, Mother Mary," Mrs. Corva said.

"You're welcome," Mother Mary replied.

"Please forgive me, Wriley. I hope you grow up to be a good man. Don't be like your father," were the last words Wriley's mother said to him before she walked out of his life forever.

"Wriley," his younger sister called out to him, but Wriley just stared at her. He watched his mother and sister leave without saying a word.

Mother Mary walked over and lovingly draped her arm around his shoulders. "I'm sorry, my dear. I know it isn't easy to separate from your family. Hopefully, with time you will feel comfortable here. Come, I will introduce you to our family. There are many kids like you here, so you will have many friends."

Wriley walked with Mother Mary outside to the courtyard where other kids were playing. There were already eighteen kids at the orphanage. Some of the more mature ones in their teens were chatting with each other while a few were reading books, and the younger ones were playing around. Wriley was not in the mood to make new friends.

"Everyone, say hi to our new family member, Wriley Corva," Mother Mary announced.

Everyone stopped and stared at Wriley. They all waved and greeted him, and one girl approached him.

"Hello, Wriley, I'm Eve," Eve introduced herself. She was two years younger than him.

"Hi," Wriley greeted softly.

"Eve was left on the doorsteps of the church on Christmas Eve as a baby, so I named her Eve Snow. She was the youngest ever to join us. She can be a great companion to you," Mother Mary introduced.

Wriley looked at Eve's sweet smile and felt sorry for her. At least he got to know his parents.

For the following days, Wriley kept to himself. He often stood near the fence looking at the cars that drove by, hoping his mother has a change of heart and return to take him home. One day, he was crying from missing his mom and sister, and then suddenly, he felt a gentle hand wiping away his tears. He turned to look at Eve.

"Don't cry. I will be your friend. Here is a flower for you." Eve handed him a gardenia she plucked from the garden. "Smell it. It smells nice," Eve brought it up close to his nose.

Wriley stared at her, slowly reached for the flower, and sniffed it as Eve smiled at him. Eve was right. The flower has a lovely fragrance. He was touched by her kindness and noticed she has a beautiful smile. From that day onward, they would hang out together. Eve introduced him to some of the other kids, and occasionally, they would play with them.

One time, as they walked around the courtyard, Wriley stopped and turned to Eve.

"Are you mad or hate your parents for leaving you?" Wriley asked.

Eve shook her head. "No, they must have their difficulties, so I don't blame them. They could have left me anywhere, but they dropped me off at the church orphanage, which shows they care for my wellbeing."

"You're too nice. I don't think I can be that forgiving."

Eve smiled. "It makes the heart lighter. That is what Mother Mary said."

"Do you wish they would come back for you one day?"

"It would be nice if they could. I always wanted to know what it feels like to live with your real family."

"When we are old enough to leave the orphanage, you and I can start our own family."

Eve's eyes widen. "Really?"

"Yes."

"Promise?" Eve held out her pinky.

Wriley crossed his pinky with hers. "Promise."

Chapter 2
Remember

Four years later, Eve and Wriley's relationship grew closer. They became best friends and often sat to draw up imaginary future lives that they would share when they grew up.

"This is going to be our house, do you like it?" Wriley showed Eve a sketch he drew.

"Yes, I love it. Can we add flowers? I want the yard to be filled with gardenias," Eve said.

"Sure, I will plant the flowers for you."

"Thank you." Eve smiled at Wriley.

One day, a couple visited the church looking to adopt a kid. They were walking with Mother Mary to observe the kids. Wriley was running to find Eve when he accidentally bumped into the woman.

"I'm sorry, ma'am," Wriley apologized.

"Oh, that is all right," Linn Hall replied.

"Here, you can have this flower," Wriley handed her one of the gardenias in his hands.

"Why, thank you," Linn accepted it graciously. His smile reminded her a lot of her late son.

"How sweet," Paul said.

"This is Wriley. He joined us four years ago," Mother Mary introduced.

"Hi, Wriley. I'm Linn, and this is my husband, Paul."

"Hello," Paul extended his hand.

Wriley shook it. "Hi."

"How old are you?" Linn asked.

"Thirteen," Wriley replied.

"Dustin would have turned thirteen this year as well," Paul said.

Wriley didn't know what was going on just stood there quietly.

"We lost our son last year due to cancer. He is the same age as you. We are looking to adopt a kid around his age. Would you like to become our son?" Linn asked Wriley.

Wriley wasn't expecting it, so he looked at Mother Mary, who smiled at him. Wriley looked back at the couple. "Really? You want to adopt me?"

"Yes, if you want to join our family," Paul replied.

"Yes, I would love to," Wriley said without hesitation.

Linn and Paul smiled. "That's great. Do you want to go with us today?" Linn asked.

"Sure. Oh wait, could you also adopt my friend, Eve? She is eleven."

Linn looked at Paul and Mother Mary.

"She is his best friend," Mother Mary explained.

"Ah, I see. You can't bear to part from her, huh?" Linn asked.

Wriley nodded his head.

"I'm sorry, Wriley, we were only planning to adopt one kid at this time," Paul placed his hand on Wriley's shoulder.

"I see," Wriley said with disappointment. "Then I want to stay here."

Linn and Paul looked at each other. "Right now, we can only afford to adopt one kid. How about you come with us now, and in the near future, we will figure out a way to adopt Eve as well," Linn reassured him.

"Really, you would do that?" Wriley asked.

Linn nodded her head. "Yes, we will come back for her, but give us some time, okay?"

"Okay," Wriley replied.

"All right, Mother Mary, please proceed with the paperwork," Paul said.

"Wonderful. Wriley, why don't you go pack your belongings and say goodbye to Eve and everyone while I get the paperwork ready for them," Mother Mary said.

"Okay," Wriley said and ran off to find Eve.

"Eve!" Wriley called out as he approached her.

Eve was reading in the courtyard, and turned to look at him.

"Here, these bloomed today." Wriley handed her the gardenias.

"Thank you, Wriley," Eve took it and sniffed the flowers. "I love the scent."

"I have some good news to tell you," Wriley shared.

Eve looked up at him.

"There is a couple that wants to adopt me."

"That's wonderful. Could they adopt me as well?"

"I did ask, but they said they can't afford two kids at this time. However, they said that they would come back for you."

"Oh," Eve was disappointed.

"Don't worry. I'll make sure they adopt you."

"It's okay if they don't want me."

Wriley grabbed her shoulders. "I promise we'll be a family. Be patient for now. I will definitely take you with me."

Eve smiled and nodded her head with complete trust in Wriley.

"I have to go pack now."

"I will help you."

"Okay."

Eve walked Wriley to the car with Mother Mary.

"This is my friend, Eve," Wriley introduced to his new parents.

"Hello, Eve," Linn and Paul greeted.

"Hi," Eve greeted them with a smile.

"You're a cute one. No wonder Wriley doesn't want to leave you," Linn teased.

Eve smiled shyly.

"Don't worry. We will eventually adopt you as well," Linn said.

"Yes, give us maybe a year," Paul said.

"Okay," Eve said.

"You're ready, Wriley?" Linn asked.

"Yes," Wriley replied.

"Let me get your bag," Paul said as he reached for Wriley's bag.

"Thanks," Wriley said and turned to Eve. "Goodbye, Eve. Take care," Wriley said as he hugged her and kissed her cheek.

Eve was surprised by the kiss but felt warm inside. "Goodbye, Wriley. Remember to come back for me."

"I will," Wriley said as he backed away.

"Here, take this flower with you," Eve handed him a gardenia.

"Thank you," Wriley said as he took the flower. "Goodbye, Mother," Wriley hugged Mother Mary.

"Goodbye, Wriley. We will definitely miss you," Mother Mary said.

"Bye," Wriley waved to Eve and Mother Mary as he climbed into the car.

"Bye Mother Mary, bye Eve," Linn waved to them as she got into the car.

"Goodbye," Paul said as he got in as well.

"Goodbye." Eve and Mother Mary waved to them.

Mother Mary knew Eve was sad to see Wriley go, so she placed her arm around Eve to comfort her. Wriley rolled down the car window, stuck his head out, and waved to them as the car drove away.

Eve ran after the car and shouted, "Don't forget me!"

"I won't!" Wriley hollered back.

Eve started to cry. She will surely miss him.

*****

Wriley enjoyed the first few months with his new parents, who loved him very much. At the same time, he misses Eve terribly every day. He dried the gardenia and sniffed it every night as he reminisced about her.

One fateful evening, as they came out from a movie theater and were on their way to the car, they were robbed at gunpoint. Linn and Paul died trying to protect Wriley.

"No, Mom, Dad? God, please save them," Wriley cried as he shook their lifeless bodies. "What did I do wrong, God? Why do you not want me to have a family?"

In one night, Wriley once again lost everything. His hope for a new and better life died with his adopted parents.

Wriley secretly followed the robber into a dark alley and hid behind a corner when he saw four other men standing around. The robber was on his knees.

"Here is the money," the robber said as he handed over the purse to a Spanish man who appeared to be the big boss.

A sidekick of the man took the purse, opened it up, and took out the money. "There are less than four hundred dollars here," Ben said. He was a bulky White man.

"You owed us six grand, remember? You said you would pay us several months ago, but you kept delaying," Jeff said. He was a slender Hispanic man.

"I'm sorry, I'll get you more in the next few days," the robber said.

"What a shame. You robbed a woman for just this much?" Javier De León, the boss, asked.

"Shouldn't gamble if you can't afford it," Jeff said.

"I'm sorry. I promise I'll give you the rest by next week," the robber promised.

"How? By robbing more people? Besides, I can't trust you anymore. It seems like you're not taking us seriously," Javier ridiculed.

Then, a muscular Black man named Diro pointed the pistol at the robber's head.

"No, no, please. I'll never do it again," the robber promised.

Wriley stepped out from the shadow where he could be seen.

"What are you doing here, kid?" Ben asked.

"I'm here to kill him," Wriley pointed at the robber.

Javier was curious and invited him over, "Come here, kid."

Wriley nervously walked over.

"What's your name?" Javier asked.

"Eli," Wriley lied.

"How old are you?" Javier asked.

"Thirteen," Wriley replied.

"Thirteen, and why do you want him dead?"

"Because he just killed my adopted parents."

"Ah, I see. I'm sorry, Eli. You scumbag, how could you kill innocent people like that," Javier gave the robber a hard punch across his face.

The robber fell over and quickly got back on his knees.

"I'm so sorry, kid," the robber apologized.

"Will that bring his parents back?" Jeff slapped his head.

"I was desperate. I'm truly sorry," the robber said.

"You want to revenge for your parents?" Javier asked Wriley.

"Yes," Wriley answered firmly.

"Good, hand him the gun," Javier ordered Diro.

"Huh?" Diro asked.

"No." The robber shook his head.

"Give him the gun. He has every right to avenge his parents. That is what a good son should do," Javier approved.

"Yes, Boss." Diro complied by handing the pistol to Wriley, who looked at it nervously before taking it.

"Take it, Eli. I'm giving you a chance to kill your enemy," Javier encouraged.

Wriley looked at the pistol for a long second before aiming it at the robber's head, who kept shaking his head.

"No, please, I'm sorry," the robber pleaded for his life.

Everyone waited patiently to see if Wriley would dare to make a move. Then, without hesitation, Wriley pulled the trigger, and a loud bang reverberated down the haunting alley, shocking everyone there.

"My boy." Javier clapped his hands, cheering Wriley's bravery.

Diro took the pistol away from Wriley as he stood there staring at the fallen body.

Javier walked over and placed his arm around Wriley. "I'm sincerely sorry about your parents. Do you have any other relatives?"

"No."

"I see. I could really use a brave soul like you. Would you like to come work for me?"

"No."

"Do you hate guys like him?" Javier pointed at the robber's body.

"Yes."

"Then this job will be perfect for you. You will get to punish bad people like him. Since you don't have any other relatives, I will take you under my wing as my son. With my protection, no one can harm you. I promise you will have a good life. You will be sitting on a pile of money."

Wriley thought it over. Being with someone was better than being on his own. Part of him wanted to go back to the church to be with Eve, but the idea of making a lot of money so he could provide Eve with a good life later trumped his decision.

"What do you say?" Javier asked.

"Come on, kid, it's a great opportunity," Diro encouraged.

"Okay," Wriley agreed.

"Great," said Javier.

"Let me bury my parents first," said Wriley.

"Oh yes, of course, we will help arrange the funeral for them. I have a daughter around your age. You two can play together," Javier said.

His parents' possession was passed to Wriley, which Javier didn't touch. Wriley was too young to be on his own, so he was willing to follow Javier for the time being as his adopted son.

Chapter 3
Forgotten

Weeks turned into months as Eve longed for Wriley every day. After a year had passed, and there was still no sign of Wriley, Eve wondered if he had forgotten about her.

Several years went by. Eve had given up hope of Wriley returning for her. She learned to accept her fate.

One day, Mother Mary saw Eve standing by the fence, looking at a gardenia in her hand. She walked over to Eve.

“Are you still waiting for Wriley?” Mother Mary asked.

Eve smiled slightly. “There is no point. He is not coming back.”

“I’m sure he has his difficulties,” Mother Mary tried to comfort her.

“Yeah, probably. It’s okay if he has forgotten about me.”

“I don’t think he has.”

“Either way, I’m fine. You don’t have to worry about me, Mother.”

“Do you want me to contact his parents?”

“No, let’s not bother them.”

“All right, then. Don’t lose hope. You never know. One day, he might show up,” Mother Mary said before walking away.

*****

All the while, Wriley was bulking up his body with kickboxing and learning the trade of his adopted father. After living with Javier for four years, Wriley has been trained to be Javier's right-hand man. Unlike Javier's men, Wriley could be quite cruel. He gets the job done and does not bullshit around. For that, he earned the respect of Javier and all of his followers.

Javier treated Wriley like his own birth son. In fact, he owed it to Wriley. From starting out as a loan shark and owning a small club with an underground gambling room in a shady corner of town, Wriley has grown Javier's business into an empire. Javier was able to purchase the largest casino in the state of New York, expand his club into the center of town, buy up more estates, and made enemies when he invaded their territories.

On the opening day at the casino, Javier happily cuts the ribbon alongside Wriley. He proudly introduced Wriley to the world "This is my son, Eli," and then hugged him tightly in front of a large cheering crowd. If Javier was the king of his empire, Wriley was the one and only qualified prince.

*****

One day, a woman walked on the sidewalk, unaware that someone had reached inside her bag and stolen her wallet. As Dean turned around to dash away, Wriley caught his arm. Dean tried to fight him, but Wriley locked his arms.

"Let go of me," Dean demanded. He was biracial, black and white, and a year younger than Wriley, now seventeen.

"You don't have to live like this," Wriley said.

"The hell, you know."

"There's a better way to make a living than stealing from innocent people."

"Yeah? If I have a job, you think I would be doing what I'm doing?"

"Come with me. I will give you a job."

"Why do you want to help me?"

"I know what it's like to have nothing."

Dean stopped struggling, so Wriley released his arms. He turned around to face Wriley. "You're really going to help me get a job?"

"Yes, now return that wallet to the woman, then follow me."

"What if she found out I stole it?"

"Just said that she dropped it."

"Okay." Dean did as Wriley suggested and ran after the woman. "Ma'am, you dropped your wallet," Dean lied as he caught up to her.

"Oh my, well, thank you, young man," the woman said with gratitude.

"You're welcome," Dean said and headed back toward Wriley.

"I'm Eli." Wriley extended his hand.

"Dean Brown." Dean shook his hand.

Wriley brought Dean home and asked Javier's permission to let Dean stay with them.

"This is my father," Wriley introduced.

"Hello, sir," Dean greeted.

"Hello," Javier greeted.

"This is my friend Dean. He doesn't have anywhere to go. I was hoping he could stay with us," Wriley said.

"You trust this kid?" Javier asked.

Wriley looked at Dean and replied confidently, "Yes."

Dean felt good that there is someone in this world who actually cares about him.

"And I trust you," Javier replied.

"Thank you, Father."

"Kat!" Javier called his housekeeper.

"Yes, sir?" Kat came down the hallway.

"Please prepare a room for our new member of the family."

"Yes, sir." Kat walked away.

"Let's go." Wriley placed his hand on Dean's shoulder.

Dean followed Wriley closely from that day and became Wriley's most trusted man.

"Thank you, Kat," Wriley said as they entered a room that's soon to be Dean's.

"Thank you, ma'am," Dean said.

"Oh, just call me Kat, and it's my pleasure," Kat said and closed the door behind her.

Dean placed his bag on the ground and turned to Wriley. "You didn't tell me your father is hella rich."

"He is my adopted father. I also work for him. If you live with us, you will also be his employee."

"What does he do? Don't tell me you guys sell drugs."

"No. Javier is a smart man. That is the one thing he stays away from. Most of his businesses are legit. He owns many properties around town, including a casino and a popular club. The rest are rented out. He is also a loan shark. My job is to make sure no one disturbs his business and collect the money when due. That's the part of Javier's business that's shady."

"I see."

"If you have any more questions, I'll be happy to answer them. For now, take a shower and join us downstairs for dinner. I'll bring you some of my clothes that you can fit."

"Thanks, man."

"You're welcome."

"Who is this guy?" Megan asked as she sat down at the dinner table. She was Javier's only daughter and the same age as Wriley. Javier's wife died giving birth to his son twelve years ago, who also passed a few days later.

"Be nice, Megan," Javier warned and turned to Dean. "Forgive my spoiled daughter."

"No problem. Hi." Dean waved to her.

"This is Eli's friend, Dean. He will be staying with us from now on," Javier introduced.

"Eli's friend? Eli doesn't have friends. He never makes friends," Megan said.

"I do now," Wriley replied.

"That's a change," Megan said caustically, but Wriley ignored her.

*****

A year has passed since Dean stayed with them. After meeting with Javier, Wriley headed back to his room. When he opened the door, he saw Megan flaunting her nude body on his bed as an invitation. Wriley immediately closed the door and walked away.

"Eli!" Megan called to no avail.

Wriley knocked on Dean's door.

"Coming." Dean opened the door. "Bro."

"I'm going to sleep in your room tonight." Wriley walked inside.

"What's wrong with your room?"

"Megan is lying naked on my bed."

"Now, I gotta see that." Dean headed for the door, but Wriley grabbed his arm and pulled him back.

"She's gonna shoot you if you open that door."

"I'm just playing." Dean smiled as he closed and locked the door.

They both lay down in bed.

"We need to move out of this place," Wriley said.

"I'll go wherever you go, bro."

*****

At least once a week, Wriley would come around the orphanage and stand from afar where he can't be seen in the hope of watching Eve walking around or playing with some of the children. Dean finally discovered his secret after tagging along with Wriley for two years.

"What is it about this place that kept you lingering here for years?" Dean asked.

"That's where my mother dropped me off, and I lived there for four years."

"I see. You must have friends there."

"Yes, there is one special person."

"Why don't you visit them?"

"I don't want her to see the version of me now."

"Ah, so it's a girl. Can you see her from here?"

"You see the one holding a white flower?"

"Yes."

"That's Eve. She was dropped off as a baby, never saw her parents. I promise her I will take her away with me one day, but I have failed to return as promised."

"It's not too late. You can still bring her out now."

"Now is not a good time, but one day for sure, I will take her with me," Wriley said as he walked away.

"You know Megan likes you a lot."

"Not my problem," said Wriley coldly.

"Boy, will she be disappointed if she finds out about Eve."

Wriley turned to Dean. "No one can know about Eve," Wriley said sternly.

"Got it," Dean promised. "Is that why you moved out? To avoid Megan?"

"That's just one of the reasons."

"How come you don't like Megan?"

"She is a spoiled brat."

"She lost her mother when she was young," Dean reminded him.

"Eve also didn't have a mother or father, but she is nothing like that."

"Eve grew up in a church. Megan grew up with a father who was a big mafia boss. What do you expect?"

"I don't care. I just know that, besides Eve, I don't have time for another woman."

"You like Eve that much?"

"Eve is one of a kind. No one can compare to her." They both got into the car.

Wriley and Dean stayed with Javier until Wriley was nineteen. Afterward, Wriley moved out, and Dean followed him. They lived together at first in the same apartment. Wriley was always cautious of Javier and wanted to keep his distance from him. Although Wriley grew up with Javier, he knew very well that living with a person like Javier was like living with a tiger. You never know when you're going to get bitten. Even though he was Javier's adopted son, it was not the same as being his own flesh and blood. Living on his own also made it easier to plan his escape with Eve.

*****

After Eve turned eighteen, Mother Mary sat down with her one day for a serious chat. Mother Mary was now in her sixties.

"Eve, you're old enough to leave the church now. Most of your friends have already left. Do you have any plans for your future?"

Eve was quiet for a moment. "I don't know where to go."

"You can apply for college. There are funds to assist students like you."

"I grew up in the church all of my life. I can't imagine being on my own. I'm afraid to be alone."

"I see. Well, what are you thinking then?"

"Can I continue to live here?

"You can, but as a nun. Are you willing?"

"All right, I will become a nun."

"It's a big decision. I want you to think it through. Don't make a haste decision because you feel like there is no other option. I don't want you to regret it later, especially when you have never had a chance to experience the real world. Don't you want to go find Wriley?"

"It has been so long. What is the use of me showing up in his life at this time? I don't want to be a burden to him. We were only friends anyway. I don't want to trouble him with our past."

"Well, I still recommend you to take time to think it over. Come to me once you are resolute."

"Thank you, Mother."

Eve spent the next few days contemplating late into the night and while walking around the campus. She thought of different possible scenarios. If she were to show up in front of Wriley now, he might act estranged toward her, or he may have a girlfriend or perhaps totally forgotten about her.

One morning, she knocked on Mother Mary's office.

"Come in," Mother Mary said.

"Good morning, Mother Mary."

"Good morning, Eve."

"I have decided. I will dedicate my life to the church."

"Very well."

Chapter 4
Vows

Since Eve grew up in the church, her postulate training period was relatively quick. After a year, Eve became a novitiate. A year later, she received her first set of vows and then her final vows at the age of twenty-three.

At Wriley's apartment, he was watering several pots of gardenias.

"I heard Eve is taking her final vows today," Dean reported as he watched Wriley.

Wriley paused for a second, then continued spraying the plants.

"Are these her favorite flowers? Is that why you have them all over your apartment?" Dean asked.

"Yes, she loves the fragrance of gardenias."

"Bro, since you love her so much, why don't you get her out already? She has become a nun. What can you do now?"

"I can still get her out."

"You going to make her break her vows?"

"I already said it before. No matter what, I will have Eve by my side."

Dean sighed. "You shouldn't have made her wait so long."

"I have my plans. I'm trying to save enough money to provide her with a good life. Besides, you think it's easy to break away from this job?"

"True, will the boss just let you leave?"

"Probably not. That's why I have developed a plan to walk away safely. At that time, I will take Eve with me. We will go somewhere far from here and start a new life."

"I see. I will support you all the way."

A couple of weeks later, Wriley decided to visit the church with Dean.

"Hello, Mr. De León. It's so nice to finally meet you," Mother Mary said as she shook Wriley's hand. It had been so long since she had last seen him. Wriley grew into a handsome, rugged man with black hair and a dark Puerto Rican complexion. With his name changed, she no longer recognized him yet saw familiarity in his eyes. Eyes that had weathered many storms and a sharp focus on one goal. Eve.

"Hello, Mother Mary. Nice to meet you as well," Wriley greeted.

"Thank you for your generous donations all these years," Mother Mary said.

"My pleasure to contribute," Wriley replied.

"You both are very kind," said Mother Mary.

"We are orphans ourselves, so we just want to give something back to the community," said Wriley.

"Yes," Dean added.

"Well, I thank you on behalf of everyone here," said Mother Mary.

"You're welcome," Wriley replied.

"Can we have a tour of the place?" Dean asked.

"Certainly, follow me," Mother Mary said as she walked them out of her office. "We have twenty-one kids here. The youngest is six, and the oldest is eighteen, and he is leaving the church soon when he starts college."

"Do most leave once they are old enough?" Dean asked.

"Yes, most do. A few lucky ones would get adopted before then. Besides, we don't have enough space to keep them all either. Occasionally, we have one that stays and becomes a religious."

"I see," Dean said as he looked at Wriley.

They walked into the courtyard where everyone was hanging out, with several of the sisters playing with the little ones, including Eve, who was now called Sister Maria.

At the sight of Mother Mary, all the sisters stopped and greeted her, and she greeted them back.

Mother Mary walked up to Eve with Wriley and Dean. Wriley eyes were fixed on Eve. He wondered if she recognized him. It had been a long time since he had been this close to her.

"This is Sister Maria. She grew up here with us. This is Mr. Eli De León and Mr. Dean Brown. They have been generous donors to the church for many years," Mother Mary introduced.

"Hello, Sister Maria." Dean waved.

Eve nodded slightly, "Hello."

"Nice to meet you." Wriley offered his palm.

"Thank you for your kindness." Eve smiled at him. She noticed his pair of green eyes were very similar to Wriley's but didn't think it was possible to be him, and since she was now a nun, she didn't dare to stare at him for too long.

Wriley missed seeing her beautiful smile. It was still the same as the first time he met her.

"It's our pleasure," Wriley said, still holding onto her hand while staring deeply into her eyes.

Eve tried to pull away, but Wriley was holding it tightly. Eve looked down at their hands, and so did Mother Mary. Dean looked at Wriley and gave him a nudge.

"Sorry," Wriley said as he let go.

Eve smiled politely.

"Would you like to see the church?" Mother Mary asked.

"Sure," Dean replied.

"This way," Mother Mary led them away.

Wriley took one last look at Eve before walking away. It seemed like she didn't recognize him, or had she forgotten about him, he wondered.

"We will come back in the near future with toys," Wriley said on the way out.

"That's very kind of you. I'm sure the children would love that," Mother Mary said.

"Thank you, Mother Mary," Dean said.

"Thank you, gentlemen."

"Goodbye," Wriley said.

"Goodbye." Mother Mary waved to them as they climbed into the car.

"You almost gave yourself away, Bro," Dean said as they drove off.

"I couldn't help it. I got lost in her eyes and smile."

"We all could see that." Dean smiled.

"It doesn't seem like she recognizes me. I wonder if she has forgotten about me."

"Could you blame her? It has been over twelve years. You're not the same kid who left."

"I will make her remember."

"How?"

"I'm planning to visit more often in the future."

"Even if you do, she is a nun now. You can't get close to her, and she may not have any feelings for you."

"I'm not letting her go."

*****

Every couple of months, Wriley and Dean would bring toys or treats to the orphanage for the following year. Wriley made many efforts to converse with Eve, but she tried to keep the conversation light and finds excuses to evade him.

One time, they offered to take everyone to the fair. While other kids were busy playing various games with Dean at the fair, Wriley approached Eve.

"Since you grew up in the orphanage, you must have a lot of childhood friends," Wriley said.

"Yes," Eve answered politely.

"Are there any particular friends you miss the most?"

Eve thought of Wriley but wasn't comfortable sharing her childhood affairs with a stranger, especially as a nun; it was inappropriate to discuss about boys. "No." Eve shook her head lightly. "Excuse me," Eve tried to escape.

Wriley watched her walk away. He wondered if she has truly forgotten about him.

Another time, they went on a field trip to the American Museum of Natural History.

"Imagine such incredible creatures once walked this earth," Wriley said as he walked up beside Eve, standing in front of the huge dinosaur fossil.

Eve glanced at him. "Yes." She smiled.

"Have you always wanted to be a nun?" Wriley asked.

Eve avoided looking at him. "Not always. I only aspired to the idea a few years ago."

"Aren't you curious about the outside world? Would you ever consider leaving the church?"

Eve looked at him with reproach for his audacious questions. "No, that thought never crossed my mind. I'll never leave the church. Pardon me." Eve nodded and walked away.

*****

"Eli and Dean have been visiting the church orphanage, bringing the kids toys and food," Ben reported to Javier at his mansion.

"He came from an orphanage. There's nothing wrong with him giving back," Javier said as he drank his wine on his sofa.

"True," Ben agreed.

*****

One day Wriley came out of the church bathroom and bumped into Eve, who was turning the corner.

"I'm so sorry," Eve said as she stabilized herself against Wriley's body.

"It was my fault. Are you alright?" Wriley asked with his arms around her.

"Yes, thank you," Eve said as she nervously backed away, but Wriley held her tight.

Eve stared at him. "Mr. De León, please."

"Eve, do you not remember me?"

Eve stared into his eyes, studied his face, and then slowly shook her head. She was afraid to say his name.

"It's me, Wriley. I have come back for you."

Eve gasped softly.

Mother Mary spotted them from afar. She had been observing Wriley for a while now and noticed that he took an interest in Eve, which worried her. "Sister Maria," Mother Mary called.

They both turned to look at Mother Mary, and Eve quickly broke away from Wriley and hurried over to Mother Mary. Her heart was pounding against her rib cage.

"Mother, I accidentally bumped into him," Eve tried to explain.

Mother Mary smiled with complete trust in her. "I know my child. I saw everything. What did he say to you?" Mother Mary asked at the same time Wriley was walking toward them. Mother Mary looked at Wriley, and Eve turned to look at him.

"Please don't blame her," Wriley pleaded.

"I wasn't blaming her. Mr. De León, we appreciate all your donations and kind gestures toward everyone, but we won't allow you to make any advances on anyone here, especially the sisters. Please respect their vows," Mother Mary rebuked.

"I'm sorry. I didn't mean to frighten Sister Maria," Wriley apologized.

"It's probably for the best that you don't come by anymore," Mother Mary advised.

"Mother, have you forgotten me?" Wriley asked, finally willing to reveal his identity.

Mother Mary stared at him for a while. "Who are you?"

"I'm Wriley. I was adopted by a couple thirteen years ago, remember?"

"Wriley?" Mother Mary asked.

"Yes, unfortunately, my parents were robbed and killed a couple of months after they adopted me. I was adopted by another man and had a name changed."

"That's terrible what happened to your parents. I'm so sorry to hear that," said Mother Mary.

"It had been years ago. I have always wanted to come back for Eve, but there were obstacles. I think now would be a good time for me to take her away."

Eve stared at Wriley while Mother Mary looked at Eve and him.

"You have to understand that Eve is now Sister Maria. She can't just leave with you," Mother Mary explained.

"I know I'm a little late. I couldn't stop her from taking her vows, but I truly wanted to be with her. Could I have a word with her alone?" Wriley asked.

"All right. Because of your past, I will make an exception for you two. I'm sure you have been waiting to catch up with her. I will leave you two to discuss the matter.

Just remember that as long as she still holds her vows, please don't challenge her."

"I understand. Thank you, Mother."

Mother Mary took one last look at the two of them before walking away.

Wriley slightly touched Eve's arm, but she quickly pulled away. "Let's go over there to talk." Wriley pointed to the courtyard.

Eve quietly followed him, and they sat down on a bench.

"Eve," Wriley started.

"Please call me by my religious name."

"All right. You don't know how long I have waited to reunite with you. You must think I have abandoned you, but there's not a single day that goes by that I don't think about you. I have finally come back for you. Are you willing to leave with me?"

Eve looked into his eyes. "I can't. I already took my final vows."

"You can always leave if you want to. This is not a prison. Your vows cannot keep you here if you don't want to stay."

"I already choose to dedicate my life to the church. I'm not going to undo the vows."

"Was it because of me?"

Eve started to tear up. "I waited every single day. Weeks turned into months, then years, and still, I waited, hoping that you had not forgotten your promise."

"I haven't."

"But you never showed up, and I had to choose between going out into the world and being on my own or staying here with the only family I have ever known. So, I have made my decision to stay. This is what I'm familiar with. This is where I belong," said Eve.

"You belong with me. I will be your family," said Wriley.

"It's too late. I had already given up that dream."

"Don't," Wriley said as he reached for her hand, which Eve pulled away.

"Please respect my vows."

"I'm sorry. Please don't give up because I never had."

"Why didn't you show up earlier? I know you have your reasons, but at least let me know that you still remember me, and I would have waited patiently until the time was right for you."

"I really wanted to, but the life I have been living is not something I'm proud of, and I don't want you to know about it. I also did it to protect you. The fewer people know about you, the safer you will be."

"I don't understand," Eve said with confusion.

"I know it may sound confusing to you right now, and I can't elaborate on the matter, but trust me, everything I did was for you. I still hold on to the promise to take you with me. Every week for the past thirteen years, I would stand at that corner looking over at the courtyard, hoping to catch a glimpse of you. Wanting so badly to run over to you, but I had to restrain myself. It's okay if you're mad and don't forgive me, but I hope you give me a chance to make it up to you."

"I was never mad at you, so there is nothing to forgive, but I can't leave with you. I will not abandon my vows. It has been so long, and we are not the same people. What if it turns out we can't get along? Where would I go then? Back to the church?"

"I'll never let you go. I'll treat you well and do whatever it takes to make you happy. I'll be patient and wait for us to get to know each other again. We will be a family. I will give you a life you have always wanted."

"I can't turn my back on God."

"Forget God. You have me now. If he were that kind, he wouldn't have all the kids abandoned at this church."

"Please don't say that. Don't insult him, don't be a sinner."

"I have lived long enough to know that there is no God, or at least when you needed him the most, he never shows up. Never did, never will."

"You must have suffered a lot after your parents passed, but you must understand that God works mysteriously."

"All right, I won't argue with you about Him. Let's talk about us. Will you come with me? You don't have to answer me right now. I will give you all the time you need to think about it. I will wait for you. However long it takes."

Chapter 5
Decision

Eve tossed and turned in bed as she replayed the words Wriley said to her. She thought back to when he kissed her cheek before leaving with his adoptive parents and how he held her earlier when they bumped into one another. Eve could feel her heart palpitating whenever she thought about him and his handsome face.

A few days later, Eve waited patiently for a penitent to finish her confession before stepping inside the confessional. As Eve entered, the old priest happened to exit, and Wriley, who had just walked into the church, jumped at the opportunity.

"Father, please hear my confession, for I have sinned. I have feelings for a man which I should not. I have waited for him for a long time, and now I've become religious, yet I cannot forget him. I can't seem to suppress this emotion inside of me," Eve confessed.

"Don't suppress it then. To have feelings is to be human. Why are you denying yourself?" Wriley asked.

Eve was startled by his voice, stood up, and left. Wriley followed after her.

"Eve," Wriley called after her.

"I'm Sister Maria now," Eve replied with irritation.

"Sister Maria," Wriley started but was interrupted.

"That was very wrong of you to listen to my confession," Eve rebuked.

"If I didn't, how could I have known how you truly felt about me?"

"It doesn't matter."

"It does."

"I'm still a nun."

"But you can always return your vows."

"Wriley, I think you should let me go because I have let go of you."

"You shouldn't lie in the house of God."

Eve stared at him, turned around, and walked away. Wriley grabbed her arm.

"Please don't touch me," Eve warned.

"Sorry, I didn't mean to upset you," said Wriley.

"I thought you said you would give me time to think things through," said Eve.

"I didn't mean to rush you. I just wanted to check on you, but it's actually an excuse to see you," Wriley tried to explain.

"This is a major decision that could change my life forever. I need more time."

"I understand. You can let me know when you have decided. Mother Mary has my number."

"Until I reach a decision, please do not come and disturb me again."

"Okay, I promise not to bother you until then."

Eve took one last look at him and walked on while Wriley slowly grinned to himself.

Mother Mary found Eve sitting in the church by herself, praying with a rosary in her hand. Mother Mary sat down next to her on the pew.

"Have you thought it through?" Mother Mary asked.

Eve shook her head. "I'm so conflicted, Mother. I don't know what to do."

"What does your heart tell you?"

"I have waited my entire life for him, but unfortunately, the timing is not right for us, and I can't bear to leave the church either."

"But do you want to be with him?"

"Yes," Eve finally admitted. "Does that make me a bad person?"

Mother Mary smiled warmly and placed her hand over Eve's. "No, my child, it does not make you a bad person nor a sinner in the eyes of God. I know how long you have hoped for Wriley to come back for you, and he finally did. I know it's much later than you expected, but it's not too late."

"But I already took my vows."

"There is a process you can go through to be relieved of your vows and go back to being a layperson."

"If I do that, I feel like I'm leaving God."

"No, my dear, God is always in your heart if you choose. He neither leaves you nor will you be far from him."

"What if I leave with Wriley and things don't work out? Will I be able to come back?"

"You can come back as a volunteer, but I believe if you don't go with him, you will live in regret the rest of your life. You're young. You should go outside and see the world for yourself. This church will always welcome you."

"This is the only home I ever knew."

"I know it's hard to leave your comfort zone. I believe Wriley will give you a good life. He hasn't given up on you all of these years. You won't find a man like that very often. Besides, I think he is determined to take you away. I can tell by the way he looks at you. He will not settle easily for a no." Mother Mary smiled.

"I'm afraid I'll be making the biggest mistake of my life."

"No, there is no such thing as a mistake, only opportunities to learn and grow. If you follow your heart, trust that it'll lead you on the right path."

"Thank you, Mother. I'll miss you and everyone here," Eve said as she threw her arms around Mother Mary.

"I'll miss you too, my dear, but I'm happy at the same time for you and Wriley."

The following day, Wriley received the good news from Mother Mary.

He anxiously answered the call. "Hello? Yes, I understand. Thank you, Mother Mary," Wriley said before hanging up the phone.

"What did she say?" Dean asked.

"Eve agreed to leave with me," Wriley said with a thrill in his voice.

Dean was excited and jumped up from the sofa. "Yes, finally!"

Wriley was smiling blissfully. "I was afraid that she would say no."

Dean has never seen him so happy. "Good thing she agreed."

A couple of days later, Wriley and Dean came to pick up Eve. Eve walked toward them with her bag of clothes after hugging Mother Mary one last time. It had been several years since Eve walked outside her room without her hair covered up. She has kept her hair short above her shoulders for ease of maintenance.

Wriley and Dean waved to Mother Mary, who waved back to them. They walked up to Eve.

"Hello," Wriley greeted.

"Hi, Sister Maria," Dean greeted.

Eve looked at them shyly. "Hi, you can just call me Eve from now on. I'm just a layperson now."

"Got it," Dean said.

"Let me help you with your bag," Wriley said as he reached for her bag.

"Thank you," Eve said.

"Oh, Bro, let me," Dean said as he grabbed the bag from Wriley and placed it in the trunk.

Wriley opened the door for Eve and gestured for her to climb in. She took one last look at Mother Mary and the church before getting in. Wriley followed after her, and Dean also got into the driver's seat and drove off.

Dean looked into the rearview mirror at Eve and Wriley and grinned to himself. He was happy for his brother. "You look even more beautiful with your hair down," Dean complimented.

"Thank you," Eve replied shyly.

Wriley has his eyes glued on her the entire time. Eve occasionally looked at him, then shyly looked away. It has been a long time since she last allowed her heart to feel anything toward men. Especially since she became a nun, she has always tried to keep her distance from them to avoid breaking her vows. Therefore, it was awkward for her to be alone in a car with two men.

*****

Wriley and Dean lived in a luxury apartment in upstate New York. They lived at the end of the hallway across from each other. The three of them stepped inside Wriley's apartment, and right away, Eve could smell the gardenia as her eyes scanned the place. Dean placed the bag on the ground.

"I will leave you two alone. If you ever need me, I live across the hall," Dean said.

"Thank you," replied Eve.

"You're welcome. Later, Bro," Dean said.

"Later," said Wriley as he picked up Eve's bag. "Follow me," Wriley said as he lead the way.

Eve followed him into the room.

"I'll help you hang your clothes," Wriley offered as he walked toward the walk-in closet.

"It's all right. I can do it by myself," Eve replied.

"Okay," Wriley said as he placed her bag down. "You can also put them in these drawers." Wriley directed her to empty drawers that he had prepared for her.

"Okay."

"Are these all of the clothes you have?"

"Yes, I haven't been wearing them for years since I usually don a habit."

"I see. I'll take you shopping tomorrow."

"I think these are plenty."

Wriley smiled. "If you live in the outside world, you will need more clothes than these."

Eve nodded her head with understanding.

"This will be your bedroom," Wriley said.

"Is there a second bedroom?" Eve asked.

"No, this is my room."

Eve nervously looked at the bed. It was already a massive change for her to be living with a male, but sharing a bed with one was something she was not ready for yet. She was still very much stuck in a nun's mindset.

As if Wriley could read her mind. "Don't worry. I'll sleep in the living room."

"I can sleep on the sofa," Eve quickly responded.

"Just sleep here. I'm used to crashing on the sofa most nights," Wriley lied.

"Okay," Eve said softly.

"I'll let you organize your stuff then. I'll be outside if you need anything."

"Thank you."

Wriley walked to the kitchen to prepare lunch while Eve put her clothes away. After a while, she came into the living room and started appreciating all the pots of gardenias around the place. Wriley quietly walked up beside her.

"You like them?" Wriley asked.

Eve looked at him. "Yes, you still remember?"

"Of course, I grew them for you."

Eve felt touched. "Thank you."

"Come, I have something to show you."

Eve followed Wriley toward a table where he had the dried gardenia that she gave him sitting in a glass terrarium.

"This is—" Eve started.

Then Wriley interjected with, "The one you gave me the day I left."

"You kept it all these years?"

"Yes. It would remind me of you whenever I look at it, and when I smell it, it feels like you're with me. I hope you know how much you mean to me."

Eve's heart was moved by his words. "I thought you had forgotten me."

Wriley took her hands. "Never, I miss you every day."

"I miss you too."

Wriley was happy to hear those words. He pulled her in and hugged her. Eve could feel her heart palpitating, and she slowly raised her arms to hug him back.

"You don't know how I long to hold you in my arms like this," Wriley said, then he looked at her. He put his hand up to touch her face and leaned in to kiss her, but Eve dodged awkwardly. "Sorry," Wriley apologized.

"No, it's just that I grew up in the church and have been a nun for several years. There are still many things I'm not used to, especially being around a man."

"I understand. I will give you time to adjust."

"Thank you."

Wriley smiled at her. "Let's have lunch."

Eve nodded her head.

The two had lunch together, catching up on old times.

"Did you ever look for your mother or sister?" Eve asked.

"No," Wriley replied.

"How come? I'm sure they would love to see you again."

"I wasn't part of their life growing up. There is no need for me to be now."

"Are you still upset at your mother?"

"No, we are just no longer a family. You are my only family."

That night, after Wriley finished using the bathroom which is located in the bedroom, he walked into the room where Eve was sitting on the bed.

"You probably go to bed early," said Wriley.

"Yes," Eve replied.

"I will close the door for you then," Wriley said as he walked toward the door.

"Thank you."

"Good night."

"Good night."

Wriley smiled and closed the door. Eve got down on her knees to pray.

*****

Wriley and Dean took Eve shopping. Eve has never gone shopping in her life and was overwhelmed by the sheer number of selections. Eve looked around for a bit but didn't know what to pick. Most of the styles were very different from those she grew up wearing. Eve turned around to Wriley.

"I don't know what to get," Eve said with her innocent eyes pleading for help.

"Let me help you choose," Wriley offered. Then he walked up and picked the outfits that he thought would look good on her.

"This would look nice," Dean said as he held up a lovely, sexy red dress.

Eve took one look at it and shook her head.

"No? Okay," Dean placed it back while Wriley smiled at him.

Wriley knew Eve probably preferred a more conservative look. “Here, try these on.” Wriley handed her a pile of clothes.

Eve grabbed them and headed to the changing room.

She came back sometime later.

“Did they fit?” Wriley asked.

“Most of them. These do,” Eve held out her left arm with the pile of clothes draping over it.

“We will take these then.” Wriley grabbed them from her arm.

Dean took the other ones from her right hand and hung them back on the rack.

“That’s a lot. Are we going to buy them all?” Eve asked.

“Yes, these are not much,” Wriley said.

“You don’t know Eve. Most girls have a huge closet of clothes,” said Dean.

“Let’s go look for other stuff,” Wriley suggested.

Dean helped Wriley carry the clothes as they walked away.

They came across the undergarment section. Eve noticed the variety of colorful bras and underwear and looked away in embarrassment. Wriley didn’t want to make it awkward for her, so he turned away and nudged Dean to walk away from the site.

“What? You’re not going to help her pick out the lingerie?” Dean teased.

Wriley gave him a stern look. “Eve is not like other girls. You have to remember that she grew up in the church orphanage and was also a nun. She is still timid toward me.”

“I know. I was just joking.”

They walked out of the department stores with several bags of clothes and shoes, which Eve thought was way more than she ever needed.

Chapter 6
Seen

Javier was playing golf while listening to updates from his men.

"Someone spotted Eli and Dean shopping with a girl," Jeff reported.

Javier paused his swing and looked at him. "Who's the girl?"

"I don't know. They didn't recognize her. Probably not one of our girls," Jeff replied.

"He has never shown interest in any girl and to go shopping with one. That's interesting. She must be someone exceptional to get Eli's attention," Javier was curious.

"I heard she seems very ordinary," Jeff said.

"Maybe ordinary is what Eli prefers," said Javier.

"Does Megan know?" Ben asked.

"We should keep it from her at this time," Javier suggested. Knowing how much his daughter was infatuated with Wriley.

"Yes, Boss," Jeff complied.

"Why hasn't he said anything to you?" Ben asked.

"I don't usually care about the women my men date."

"But he is like a son to you."

"He must have his reasons. If he wants me to know about her, he will tell me in time."

*****

After shopping, the three went home, and Dean returned to his place.

Eve and Wriley were sitting on the sofa watching TV.

"Should I go to school or look for a job?" Eve asked.

"Why?" Wriley asked.

"I can't just live with you and have you take care of me for the rest of my life."

"I'm willing and can take care of you forever. You don't have to worry about making money. I make plenty enough."

"What exactly do you do?"

"My job is complicated."

"It must be a good job since you get paid so well."

"Yes, it makes good money, but it could be dirty at times."

"You don't work every day?"

"Not so much anymore, only when I'm needed."

"I see," Eve could tell that Wriley didn't want to talk about his job as he evaded the topic several times.

"Are you bored staying home all day?" Wriley asked.

"Usually, there is always something to do when I'm at church. There's private prayer time, mass, sermon, taking care of the kids, and helping with other tasks."

"Now that you have more free time, what would you like to do?"

"I'm not sure."

"Do you like to read, watch TV, play any sport, or do arts and crafts?"

"I like to read."

"I will get you a collection of books, and you can read them one by one."

"Okay, thank you."

"You're welcome. On my next break, I'll take you to travel the world. You won't be bored for long."

"Can I go back to visit the church sometime?"

"Of course, just let me know when you want to go, and we can take you."

"Okay."

"Do you want to go for a walk?" Wriley knew she must be bored staying indoors all day, so he wanted to take her out for some fresh air.

"Sure."

As Eve was out walking with Wriley, they were spotted by unwanted eyes. With his line of work, Wriley has made numerous enemies throughout the years.

"Hey, isn't that Eli?" Scott asked.

"Yeah, and he is with a girl," Darel said.

"I've never seen him with a girl before," Scott said.

"He probably just started seeing her," Darel said.

"I have wanted to get him back for our boss," Scott said.

"Yeah, I can't forget how he embarrassed us that time at the club," Darel said.

Their boss, Seth Marsh was a business rival of Javier. The two had long-budded heads but kept their cool as long as no one stirred troubles.

Wriley reached for Eve's hand. Eve looked around, feeling embarrassed as she was not used to holding hands with a man in public, and pulled away gently. Wriley looked at her. "You're still shy toward me?"

"I'm sorry." Eve felt bad.

"That's all right. What can I do to make you more comfortable around me, like when we were kids again?"

"It had been years ago. Please give me more time."

Wriley nodded his head with understanding as the two kept walking.

"Eve, now that we live together, I want you to be completely honest with me. Please talk to me whenever you are sad, upset, or have any concerns. Don't hide your emotions from me. I won't know how to help you unless I know what is going on, and I hate to have you suffer alone. You only have me here, so you can come to me for anything."

"Okay."

"Tomorrow, I'll take you sightseeing."

"Sure."

*****

They left before dawn and arrived at the breathtaking view of Niagara Falls.

"Picturesque, isn't it?" Wriley asked.

"Yes, very majestic. It's amazing all the wonders God created," Eve commented.

Wriley was glad that she was enjoying it.

"Bro, let me take a pic of you two," Dean suggested.

"Okay," Wriley gave permission.

"Closer, sis, don't be a stranger," Dean teased.

Eve looked at Wriley shyly before moving closer to him.

“Bro, must I direct you? Put your arm around Eve,” Dean instructed.

Wriley did it slowly so as not to fright Eve.

“Good,” Dean approved. “Look more lovey-dovey.”

“Would you just hurry up and take the photo,” Wriley was getting agitated for Eve’s shake.

“Okay, okay. There, lovely,” Dean said.

They hung around the area the rest of the day and headed back in the evening. Eve fell asleep on the late ride home. Wriley took off his jacket to cover her and rested her head on his shoulder. Eve aroused just as they parked the car.

“We’re home,” Dean announced.

Eve looked up, surprised to see herself leaning on Wriley’s chest.

“You’re up?” Wriley asked.

“Yes.” Eve sat up.

“If you’re sleepy, I’ll carry you upstairs,” Wriley offered.

“I’m fine. I’m awake now.” Eve handed Wriley his jacket.

“Okay.” Wriley put his jacket back on.

They got out of the car and headed toward the elevator when Eve tripped on her foot.

Wriley caught her. “Are you alright?”

“You, okay?” Dean asked.

“Yes. Thank you,” Eve replied.

“Here, let me carry you.” Wriley lifted her into his arms.

“I can walk.”

"It's way past your bedtime; you must be drowsy. Just let me carry you."

"Just take advantage of it, sis. I would if he is willing to carry me," Dean joked.

Eve smiled shyly.

Wriley enjoyed having her in his arms as they headed back to their apartments.

*****

The evening of the following day, Wriley handed Eve a big gift box.

"This is for you," Wriley said.

"Thank you." Eve wondered what the occasion was.

"Please put these on. I want to take you out for a nice dinner tonight."

"Okay." Eve now understood as she walked into the bedroom to change.

She returned later in an elegant dress that was not too revealing that Wriley had picked out while holding a pair of heels in her hand.

"You look beautiful, Eve," Wriley complimented as he walked toward her.

"Thank you. I've never worn shoes this high before?" Eve showed him the heels.

"I know. You're probably not used to it yet. Here, sit down. Let me help you wear them." Wriley guided Eve to the sofa, then crouched in front of her and slid the heels onto her feet one foot at a time. "Okay, let's try standing up." Wriley held her hands and pulled her up.

Eve nervously took a step in those uncomfortable heels.

"Are they comfortable? If not, we can throw them away, and you can wear whatever shoes you like."

Eve didn't want to waste it. "They're fine."

"Okay, you can hold on to my arm for support." Wriley wrapped her arm around his.

Eve nodded, and they headed for the door with Dean waiting in the hallway.

"Wow, sis. You look gorgeous. Hardly recognize you," Dean complimented.

"Thank you."

"I'll be around. Just call me when you're ready to head out," Dean said as he dropped them off at a fancy restaurant.

"Okay," Wriley said as he got out.

"Thank you, Dean." Eve waved to him.

"Enjoy your night." Dean drove off.

As they entered the place, Eve felt many eyes on her and Wriley. Eve knew this was not a simple restaurant where the common folks would go to eat. It was for people with money to spare.

"How's the food?" Wriley asked.

"Good, but isn't this place expensive?"

Wriley smiled. "You don't have to worry about it, Eve. I want you to enjoy the best of this world."

"But I don't need all these things."

"I know you don't, but this is what I wish to offer to you. I have worked hard all these years to make sure I can do that."

"Wriley."

"Eve, there are so many more places that I want to show you, and we'll have all the time to do so."

"Mhm." Eve smiled and nodded.

The following day, Eve approached Wriley, sitting on the sofa.

"I need to go buy some personal items," Eve said nervously as she sat beside him.

"What do you need? I'll tell Dean to get it for you."

Eve shook her head. "I should go. It's female hygiene stuff."

Wriley understood. "Okay, let's go. Dean can take us."

Eve nodded, and they both stood up.

Dean drove them to a nearby convenience store.

"I can go in alone," Eve said.

"I'll go in with you. Dean, you can stay here. We'll be quick."

"Okay," Dean replied.

Wriley and Eve walked inside the female products aisle. Eve looked at all the different selections and wasn't sure what to choose.

"Which brand do you usually use?" Wriley asked as he saw her hesitation.

"I don't know. The church provides them, so I never had to buy them."

"I see. Excuse me, miss." Wriley turned to a middle-aged woman standing nearby.

"Yes?" The woman turned toward them.

"My girlfriend is not familiar with all the products. Could you recommend her something?"

Eve was shy at the word girlfriend.

"Oh. Uhm, have you used tampons before?" The woman asked Eve.

Eve shook her head.

"Would you like to try?"

Eve shook her head again.

"Okay, well, if you just want pads, this is the kind I usually use. They are very light and comfortable." The woman pointed to a brand of flexible pads with wings. "You're tiny, so you probably want to get size one or two."

"We'll take this then." Wriley grabbed two boxes. "Thank you," he said to the woman.

"No problem. I think that's so sweet of you to go shopping with your girlfriend."

Wriley smiled. "Thanks. Is there anything else you need?" Wriley asked Eve.

Eve shook her head.

"Okay, let's go," Wriley said to Eve with his hand on her back.

"Thank you," Eve said to the woman before following Wriley.

"You're welcome." The woman smiled at Eve. After they walked away, the woman was grinning to herself. "Such a cute couple."

After Wriley paid at the cash register, the cashier handed him the bag.

"Thank you," Wriley said.

"Have a nice day," the female cashier said as she envied Eve for having such a handsome and caring boyfriend.

"You too," Wriley said and walked outside with Eve.

"All done?" Dean asked as they climbed into the car.

"Yes," Wriley replied.

Wriley handed Eve the bag after they stepped inside the apartment. "Here you go."

"Thank you." Eve grabbed the bag and walked to the bedroom.

"That's so manly of you, Bro," Dean praised.

"Shut up," Wriley thought Dean was making fun of him.

"I'm serious. Not many guys would be willing to go buy those things. Eve is a lucky girl. I'm sure Boss and the guys would kill to see this. I wondered what they would think of you."

"Go back to your place."

Dean laughed. "Alright. See you later, Bro."

A few days later, Javier called Wriley and Dean to his place for a chat and an assignment. As soon as Wriley stepped inside the mansion, Megan flew toward him with her arms extended.

"Eli!" Megan threw herself at him, but Wriley took a step back as Dean intercepted the hug.

"Hi, Megan," Dean greeted.

Megan quickly pushed him away. "Go away, Dean."

"Aren't you happy to see me?" Dean teased.

"No." Megan moved toward Wriley and insisted on hugging him. "It's been a while since I have seen you."

Wriley pulled her arms down from his neck. "I've been busy lately."

"Is it because my father gave you too many tasks? I can tell him to give you less."

"No, I'm busy with my own stuff."

"Oh, what kind of stuff?"

"It's my personal business."

"Fine, if you don't want to tell me. I miss you. You don't come here often anymore. I'm still waiting for you."

"Megan, I told you already. You're just like a little sister to me. I don't have any other feelings for you."

"I don't care. I love you, and I won't date anyone else."

"I'm available," Dean interjected.

"Who cares about you," Megan said.

"Don't have to be so mean," Dean joked.

"I don't have time for your spoiled princess mood. I have to see Father." Wriley walked away.

"Bye." Dean hurried after Wriley.

"Eli!" Megan called, but Wriley ignored her. "If I can't have you. No one can."

"Guess it's a good idea to keep Eve a secret," Dean said to Wriley.

"You think?" Wriley replied.

"Megan is crazy for you."

"I wish she could find a new target."

"At least Javier doesn't force you to go out with her."

"He can't. He would regret it if he did."

*****

A week later, they paid a visit to the church, bringing snacks for the kids. Mother Mary and everyone were happy to see them, especially Eve. The little kids ran up to hug Eve.

Eve had a private chat with Mother Mary while Wriley and Dean played with the kids.

"How is life on the outside?" Mother Mary asked.

Eve smiled. "Very different."

"How does he treat you?"

"He is very kind and patient toward me."

"That's good."

"I'm still a bit hesitant to get close to him. I guess I'm not used to being around a man."

Mother Mary smiled. "After some time, you will get used to living among them."

"I hope so."

"But are you happy being with him?"

"Yes."

"He is not pressuring you, is he?"

Eve shook her head. "No, he is very respectful of me."

"That is how it should be. He seems like a gentleman. He grew up to be a fine young man. I'm glad he came back for you and truly happy for you both."

"Thank you, Mother."

After the three of them drove off, a man approached Mother Mary.

"Hello," he greeted her.

"Hello, can I help you?" Mother Mary asked.

"One of the gentlemen earlier looked familiar to me. Is his name Eli?"

"Yes."

"Does he come here often?"

"Occasionally, he used to live here for a couple of years as a kid, so he is returning now to donate and bring gifts for the children."

"I see. That is very nice of him."

"Yes, indeed."

"What about the lady that accompanied him? She also looks familiar, but I don't know her name."

"Ah, if you have attended the service here, you may know her as Sister Maria. She also grew up in this orphanage with Eli. She is now relieved of her vows and goes back to being Eve. They were close since they were kids, so Eli has come back to take her with him."

"I see. No wonder she looks familiar. Thank you."

"You're welcome."

"Have a good day."

"You as well."

The man turned to walk away.

Scott and Darel were sitting nearby in their car and heard the conversation.

"So she is his long-lost love," Darel said.

"And a nun as well, very interesting," Scott added.

"No wonder she seems different than other women."

"Eli with a nun, now that is the funniest thing ever."

"Yeah." The two men laughed.

*****

Ben reported what he had learned in Javier's office at his mansion.

"So, she is his childhood sweetheart," Javier commented.

"Seems like it," Ben said.

"A nun?" Jeff asked.

"She is relieved of her vows," Ben replied.

"Well, good for him to reunite with her," Javier said.

"I wonder why he waited so long," Jeff asked.

"He probably wanted to make sure he has a stable life before bringing her out," Javier said.

"Make sense," Jeff said.

Suddenly, Megan busted into the room. "Eli has a girl?"

"Now, Megan," Javier tried to calm her.

"No wonder why he turned me down. I want to know who she is and what she looks like. What is so great about her?"

"She is nothing compared to you, Megan," Jeff said.

"It doesn't matter who she is. They have known each other since they were kids. You can't compete with that," Javier said.

"But Dad, you know how much I love Eli, but he has refused me all these years. I want to know if she is worth it."

"You shouldn't be bothered with those kinds of things. Worth it or not is for Eli to decide."

"I won't give up so easily. Aside from Eli, I won't marry anyone else."

"There are better men out there than Eli," Ben said.

"I don't care. I just want him."

"You are to leave him alone and his girl as well. Eli is not to be messed with," Javier ordered.

"Humph." Megan left the room.

"Poor Megan," Ben said.

"Make sure she doesn't do anything stupid," Javier ordered.

"Yes, Boss," Ben and Jeff replied.

Chapter 7
Fragile

Javier has another assignment for Wriley.

"Dean and I have to go to work again today. We will be back in a couple of hours," Wriley shared.

"Okay," said Eve.

"If you need anything, call me," Wriley instructed.

"I will," replied Eve.

"You have all these books to read now," said Wriley.

Eve looked at the several boxes of books that Wriley had ordered for her and smiled. "Yes, thank you for getting me all of these books."

"You're welcome. I'll see you later."

"Bye."

"Remember, don't open the door for strangers."

"I know."

Wriley walked out and closed the door behind him. Eve returned to organizing the books on the bookcase that Wriley just bought as well.

Scott and Darel watched with two other men from their car, waiting for Wriley and Dean to drive off.

"Do you have experience being with a girl?" Wriley asked during the car ride.

Dean looked at him. "You mean sleeping with them?"

"Yeah."

Dean started to laugh and said, "Bro, must you ask?"

"I'm regretting it now," said Wriley.

Dean continued to laugh. "You and Eve are the same. So innocent when it comes to relationships."

"Forget I ask."

Dean tried to stop laughing. "I'm sorry. What do you want to know?"

"Does it hurt them?"

"Oh, I see, you're asking for Eve."

"No, just answer the question."

"Well, it depends. Some are more sensitive than others, usually only with their first time. It may be a little uncomfortable, but it should be fine if you take it slow. It will also help if you massage the area. That would stimulate them and loosen them up; then, it won't hurt. After they get used to it, they will enjoy it even more than men. But if we are talking about Eve, you might want to be extra gentle."

"I'm always gentle with her."

"I know. You treat her very differently compared to how you interact with others. I hope she knows how special she is to you."

"I don't care if she knows. I just want her to be happy."

"Wait, so you two haven't?"

"She doesn't even let me hold her hand."

"Huh? That reserved? Haven't you been sleeping in the room with her?"

"No, I sleep on the sofa."

"Oh, Bro, you got a long way to go. I guess that's what happens when you date a nun. Do you need me to teach you some moves?"

Wriley gave him a look. "You seem to have a lot of experience with women, don't you?"

"Need you say?"

"How many women have you been with?"

"I don't know, Bro. I don't keep count of that stuff. Maybe a couple. They are mainly girls down at the club."

"You're not serious with any of them?"

"No, whenever they want something more, I have to let them go because I can't offer that to them at the moment. I do envy what you have with Eve."

"Do you regret following me?"

"No, never. If it weren't for you, I would still be sleeping on the streets or in some prison. You gave me a life."

"I'm glad you don't regret it. I'm afraid Eve will regret being with me."

"I'm sure she appreciates your efforts toward her."

"It doesn't matter what I do. She is not used to being around men yet. I guess I will have to be more patient with her."

"Don't worry. Eventually, she will warm up to you."

"Are you planning to find someone nice and settle down?"

"I want to, but like you, I don't think it's a good time to drag her into my world. Once you leave with Eve, I will follow you as well. Then I will settle down."

"That's good."

*****

Eve heard the doorbell ring. She remembered Wriley said not to open the door to strangers, but then a voice called out, "Service staff."

Eve opened the door to see Scott, Darel, and two other men.

"Hello, Sister Maria," Darel mused.

Eve immediately felt uneasy and quickly closed the door, but her strength was no match for them as they busted their way in.

"Who are you, people? What do you want?" Eve asked as she backed away.

"Well, we came by to play with your boy, but you'll do since he is not home," Scott said as they slowly approached her.

"Please, no," Eve shook her head and then ran for the bedroom, but Darel caught up to her and grabbed her.

Eve screamed. "Please let me go!"

"Don't be scared, Sister," Scott said.

"Help! Help! Wriley, help me!" Eve started to scream at the top of her lungs, but Darel covered her mouth.

They dragged her into the bedroom and threw her onto the bed.

Eve continued to plead with them. "Please don't, please," Eve started to cry.

"Shh...don't cry. If it wasn't your man giving us a hard time, we wouldn't be doing this to you. You only have Eli to blame," Scott said.

"I don't know what he did, but I'm sorry. Please let me go," Eve cried.

"We can't. We want to leave a present for Eli," Scott said as he walked over, grabbed her blouse, and tore it open.

"No! Help! Wriley!" Eve cried out.

*****

After Wriley and Dean collected the money, they headed home.

"That was easy," Wriley said.

"That's because they are afraid of you, Bro. That's why the boss sent you. No one dares to turn you down."

*****

Eve was lying naked on the bed with Eli's name etched into her back.

"Hurry, we got to go," Darel said.

"Wait, we haven't had fun with her yet. I always wanted to fuck a nun," Scott said.

"We don't have time today. Eli can be back any moment. We are dead if he catches us here. Come on," Darel urged.

"Fine, another time then. Bye, Sister Maria, tell Eli we said hi," Scott said.

The four men hurried and exited the place.

As Wriley and Dean pulled up in front of the apartment, they saw the four men walking out.

"Wait, those guys look familiar. Aren't they Seth's men?" Dean asked.

"Yeah," Wriley said as he got out of the car.

"What are they doing here?" Dean asked.

Wriley paused and looked up at the building, and it dawned on him. "Eve!" Wriley called out as he dashed inside the building, with Dean following close behind.

They entered the apartment and ran toward the bedroom.

"Eve!" Wriley called out.

At the bedroom entrance, they could see Eve's nude body lying on her stomach across the end of the bed with her face toward them. Dean quickly turned away from the shocking sight.

Wriley was devasted as he dragged his feet toward her while Eve slowly slid her body off the bed, pulling the blanket to cover her front side. Dean respectfully closed the bedroom door after Wriley went inside.

Wriley knelt in front of her. "Eve," he spoke softly.

Eve couldn't say a word as she let the tears rolling down her cheeks tell it all.

"I'm so sorry, Eve. I shouldn't have left you by yourself," Wriley said as he ever so gently touched her arm as if she were a fragile piece of glass.

Eve shrank her body away from his hand. Wriley can't imagine how broken Eve must feel right now. He didn't know how to comfort her or make her pain disappear. He looked behind her back and saw blood dripping. He clenched his fist, wanting to kill everyone involved in this.

"Eve, let me take you to the hospital, where you will get the appropriate care."

Eve shook her head lightly. Wriley took off his jacket, placed it around her back, and sat facing her. He was as distraught as she was.

"Let me help you then."

Eve shook her head again. Wriley was at his wits' end. He was afraid if he touched her, she would shatter into pieces.

God, why must you do this to her? Wriley asked in vain.

Wriley sat there for an hour staring at Eve, who refused to move or speak.

“Please say something. It scares me to see you like this. I’m usually not scared of anything, but I’m scared of losing you,” Wriley said as he wished he knew what was going on in her mind.

Eve continued to give him a blank stare. She wondered if it was a mistake to leave the church and whether God was punishing her.

“Eve, please let me address your wounds. Otherwise, it may get infected.”

Eve finally responded to him. “I want to shower first.”

Wriley was glad she finally spoke. “Sure, let me help you up.”

Wriley helped Eve wrap the bed cover around her body, then carefully picked her up and carried her to the bathroom.

“Do you need me to help you?” Wriley asked as he set her down.

Eve shook her head.

“I will be outside if you need me,” Wriley said before walking out and closing the door.

Wriley got out the medical kit and set it on the bedside drawer. He also got out another bed cover and spread it over the bed, awaiting Eve.

Eve came out half an hour later with a bathrobe on. She slowly walked over to Wriley, who met her halfway.

“Come lay on the bed,” Wriley said.

Eve sat down on the bed.

"You will have to take off the robe. You can cover yourself with a blanket. I won't look," Wriley said as he turned around.

Eve went under the cover, removed her robe, and tossed it on the ground.

"Are you ready?" Wriley asked after giving her enough time.

"Yes," Eve replied as she made herself comfortable with her back facing up.

Wriley turned around and sat on the bed. He slowly pulled down the blanket, just far enough to review the entire wound and begin to address it.

Eve flinched as the cotton tip contacted the raw skin even though Wriley tried his best to dap on the site gently.

"I'm sorry, Eve, just bear with it a little longer."

Afterward, he taped a big gauze over the wound.

"It's done. Let me get you pain medication."

Eve shook her head. If God wanted her to experience this, she must bear the pain.

"Is there anything else I can do for you?"

Eve shook her head again.

"Eve, did those men do anything else to you?"

"No," Even replied softly.

Wriley felt some relief. "Get some rest. I will be outside," Wriley said, then walked out.

Dean stuck around, waiting anxiously on the sofa for the past two hours.

"How is she?" Dean asked.

Wriley shook his head as he dropped onto the sofa opposite Dean. Wriley ran his hands over his face. "I don't know if she will ever heal from this."

"That bad?"

"Those bastards carved my name on her back."

"Fucking low lives using Eve to get back at you because they are too cowardly to face you head-on."

"It will leave a significant scar on her back, but it's the scar in her heart that I'm worried about. I'm afraid she will not want to be by my side anymore and will turn away from me completely. She refused to let me take her to the hospital and just sat in silence for over an hour before she let me address her wounds. She is so fragile right now. I don't know what to do for her. It feels as if she will fall apart with one touch."

"She must be so traumatized. I'm sorry, Bro. We will get revenge for her."

"I'm going to kill everyone who touched her, every single one of them."

"When?"

"I have to wait for Eve to heal first. I can't go anywhere with her in this state, and I don't feel safe leaving her alone again."

"We can't take her everywhere with us. Why not let the boss know so he can send us some bodyguards to protect her?"

"No, I don't want him to know about her. If he finds out that she is the reason I'm leaving, then he will use her against me to make me stay."

"I see. Besides carving on her back, did they—"

Wriley knew what Dean was about to ask and replied, "No."

"That's good." Dean nodded.

"What they have done is terrible enough."

"I agreed, but I'm glad they didn't go all the way."

"Eve wouldn't be able to take it if they did. That would destroy her."

"Those sons of bitches deserve to die."

After a moment of sitting there in silence, Wriley stood up. "I will stay in the room with her tonight so she can feel safe."

"That's a good idea. I will sleep here tonight just in case."

Wriley quietly entered the room and saw Eve had fallen asleep. He carried a chair over to the bedside and sat down. Wriley stared at her late into the night as he blamed himself for taking her out too soon, for not being careful enough to hide her from his enemies, and for leaving her unattended. Now, he must change his plan and find a way to get her far away from here as soon as possible before more danger headed their way. Wriley finally drifted into his sleep.

Two hours later, he was woken up by Eve's voice.

"No, please, don't hurt me. Don't touch me. Wriley, help," Eve talked in her sleep.

Wriley gently touched her shoulder. "Eve, Eve," Wriley called softly.

Eve opened up her eyes and turned her head to face Wriley. "Wriley," Eve called his name.

"I'm here. That was just a nightmare. You're safe now," he stroked her head with his left hand.

Eve started to cry. "I called out your name, but you never showed up to rescue me."

Wriley kneeled beside the bed and held her hand with his right hand. “I’m so sorry, Eve. I was too far away. If I were around, I would have never let them touch you.”

Eve continued to cry. “I think God is punishing me for giving up my vows.”

“No, don’t think like that. If anything, he should be punishing me for taking you away. It is not your fault. Everything is my fault. Don’t ever blame yourself. I promise I will protect you well from now on. I won’t let another person lay a finger on you.”

“You were late again,” Eve shook her head.

“Eve, please don’t leave me. I spent all these years waiting for you. I don’t know how to live if I don’t have you in my life. I know you feel broken inside. Give me time to mend it. The future will be better, trust me.”

“I have always trusted you, but you have let me down.”

“I know I don’t deserve to be with you, but Eve, I love you too much to let you go. I will shoulder any punishment God sends our way. I will never let you get hurt again. Just don’t leave me.”

Eve looked into his eyes, not knowing what else to say. She wanted to stay with him, but his secret world was starting to reveal itself.

Chapter 8
Stay

Eve awoke to find Wriley sleeping in a sitting position next to the bed, holding her hand. She stared at him, feeling tormented inside.

After Wriley woke, he redressed her wound before she got out of bed.

"I will bring breakfast to you once you get ready," Wriley said and walked toward the door.

"Good morning, Bro. I made you two breakfasts," Dean greeted.

"Thanks." Wriley sat down at the dining table.

"Is sis going to join us?"

"She is getting dressed. I'll bring the food to her after I eat."

"How is she doing this morning?" Dean asked as he sat down.

"Hard to say. She woke up from a nightmare last night, and we had a chat. It seems like she can't trust me to protect her anymore. I can't trust myself to keep her safe either."

"Don't say that, Bro. Once we kill those guys, it will be over."

"There will still be others that want to come after me. I can't kill them all or fast enough. I must take her away as soon as possible."

"Yeah, do that. Just tell me what you want me to do."

Wriley knocked on the bedroom door.

"Come in," Eve said.

Wriley entered the room with a food tray and placed it on the bed. Eve was sitting up, fully dressed.

"Thank you," Eve said.

"Dean prepared it."

"Please thank him for me."

"I will. Is your back hurting?"

"A little."

"Let me get you medicine to take."

"It's fine. I can handle it."

"I don't want you to have to bear the pain."

"I'm okay, really."

"All right," Wriley said as he sat down on the bed facing her.

"Who were those men? Why were they looking for you?"

Wriley didn't want to answer her questions but knew he owed her an explanation. "Their boss and my boss don't get along. One time I kicked them out of the club for being disruptive toward the dancers, and they held a grudge against me since."

"They seek revenge just over that?"

"At that time, I gave them a beaten."

"You hurt them?"

"That's because they started wrecking things. That's the only way to get them to stop."

"Is that your job? Working at the club?"

"My job entails many things. It's my boss's club, so I help him manage it at times."

"Can you find another job where you won't have to deal with such conflicts?"

"My boss is also my adopted father. I owe him a lot, so I help him whenever I can."

"I see," Eve looked down at her food.

"It will not be forever, though. I plan to resign in the near future and take you somewhere far away where we will have a more peaceful life."

"Really?" Eve looked up at him.

"Yes. That has always been my plan for you. That is why I waited until I saved enough to take you away. Does this mean you agree to stay with me?"

Eve contemplated for a long second before nodding her head slightly, and Wriley smiled with relief.

After Wriley dressed her wounds at night, he settled down in the chair next to the bed. Eve turned around to look at him.

"You're going to sleep on the chair again?"

"Yes, I'll stay here in case you need anything."

"I will be fine. You should go lie down. It's uncomfortable to sleep like that."

"It's not that bad. I'm used to it. I want to be by your side so you can feel safe."

"I feel safe now. You don't have to worry about me."

"How about I sleep on the ground? Can I do that?"

Eve thought for a second. "If that's what you want."

Wriley smiled as he stood up and pulled the chair away. Then walked over to the other side of the bed to grab a pillow and an extra blanket. He set up next to the bed to be close to Eve. Eve watched him, and once he lay down, she turned to face the opposite direction.

"Wriley?"

"Yes?"

"Why do you want to be with me?"

Wriley lay on his right arm, facing the bed. "You're the first and only person who came to talk to me when I first arrived at the orphanage. You left me with an unforgettable impression when you handed me a flower, and I find comfort in your smile. I thought you were the most beautiful thing in the world."

"You lived outside for thirteen years. I'm sure you have met many wonderful women. Why did you come back for me, someone who is so naive to the outer world?"

"Because you're not like anyone else. You have a pure heart and see the goodness in everything. You're the light in my dark world. I don't care about other women. I just know that you're the only person I want to be with and want to protect my whole life."

"What if I'm not worth all your efforts?"

"You're worth more than anything in this world."

"What if I can never become like other women in society."

"I don't want you to be like them. I love you because you are you, and I will patiently wait for you to be comfortable with me."

Eve was moved by his words.

She decided to join them for breakfast. Wriley and Dean heard the door open and turned to look. Wriley got up and walked over to Eve.

"What do you need?" Wriley asked.

"Nothing, I'm just going to have breakfast," replied Eve.

"I can bring it inside for you," Wriley offered.

"It's all right. I can move around just fine, so you don't have to keep bringing me food," said Eve.

"That's good that she wants to join us instead of being locked up in the room all day," Dean said.

"Come, then," Wriley held her arm and led her to the table. He pulled out the chair for her, and Eve sat down.

"Good morning, sis," Dean greeted her.

"Good morning. Thanks for preparing all those meals."

"You're welcome. Hopefully, my cooking is not too terrible."

"You're a good cook," Eve complimented him with a smile.

"Thank you. Hear that, Bro?" Dean joked.

Wriley smiled. He was glad Eve felt comfortable enough to come out of the room today.

In the evening, Eve came out of the bathroom and walked toward Wriley, who was waiting for her.

"Are you ready?" Wriley asked.

Eve looked down and slowly unbuttoned her pajamas in front of Wriley. Wriley nervously watched her, unsure if he should turn away, but then he thought Eve must know what she was doing. Eve slid her shirt down toward half of her back, bearing her chest, then turned around so Wriley could dress her wounds. Wriley stood still to take in what just happened and what it meant for their relationship. When he came to his senses, he started peeling off the old gauze.

Afterward, Wriley carefully pulled up her shirt over her shoulders. Eve started buttoning her shirt while Wriley put the supplies away.

"Thank you," Eve said.

"I'm supposed to take care of you. You shouldn't have gotten hurt in the first place. It's all my fault."

Eve turned around to face Wriley. "I don't blame you," she said.

"I'm so grateful that you're giving me another chance. I was terrified that you may leave me," said Wriley

"I don't have anywhere else to go. You're my only home."

Wriley grabbed her hands. "Eve, I'll never let you suffer again."

"Mhm." Eve nodded.

He looked at her with his heart about to jump out of his chest. "If you need anything, come get me. I'll be sleeping outside tonight."

"Okay."

"Good night."

"Good night."

Eve watched Wriley walk out.

Dean looked up at Wriley when he saw the door open.

"I'm going to sleep out here tonight," Wriley announced.

"Why? Did she kick you out?" Dean asked.

"No, I wanted to."

"Did you see something you shouldn't?" Dean teased.

"No."

"Bro, why you look so flustered? What happened?"

"Nothing," Wriley said as he gulped down a full glass of water.

"Something must have happened. Your face is turning red."

"Stop being so nosy," Wriley said as he lay down on the sofa.

"Probably peeped at her."

Wriley heard it and threw a pillow at him. "Shut up and sleep."

"Definitely did," Dean mumbled and grinned to himself. He was curious about what happened behind that door and could only let his imagination run wild.

Wriley replayed the scene and wondered if this meant Eve was warming up to him. Wriley turned to his side and forced himself to go to sleep.

Chapter 9
Bleed

Eve's wounds healed well a month later, although the scars were noticeable. Wriley continued to apply medicine on her back to minimize the marks as much as possible.

"I'm sorry about the huge scars on your back," Wriley said after he finished applying the ointment.

Eve buttoned up her shirt and turned to face him. They were both sitting on the bed.

"It's okay, as long as it doesn't hurt anymore and you don't mind it."

Wriley held her hands. "I don't mind it. No matter what happens, I will always love you the same. Nothing can make me love you less," Wriley said as he started to touch her face.

Eve gazed into his eyes and touched his hand. "I believe you." Eve smiled.

Wriley pulled her into his chest and held her. "Eve, tomorrow I will take you to a place with us. It will be dangerous, so I need you to be careful."

Eve looked at him. "Where are we going?"

"I can't tell you, but this is to keep you safe so that those men can never hurt you again."

"Can't we just contact the police?"

"No, I will have to handle this matter myself."

"What are you planning to do? I don't want you to get hurt."

"Don't worry. I will be fine. Just do as I say, okay?"

"Okay." Eve couldn't help but worry about what Wriley planned to do. She was still very much clueless about his work.

*****

Dean pulled the car up in front of the bar where Seth's men usually hang out.

"Eve, stay in the car and lie down so no one will see you. Don't step outside, understand?" Wriley instructed.

Eve nervously nodded her head.

"Don't worry, sis, we will be out soon," Dean said before getting out of the car.

"Everything will be okay," Wriley gave her a comforting smile before getting out.

Eve did as instructed and lay down on the back seat, waiting anxiously.

Dean and Wriley busted into the place and started shooting at everyone in sight.

Eve jumped at the first few sounds of gunshots. "Wriley." Eve voiced with concern, contemplating whether she should check on him, although he instructed her to stay.

The other side also fired back. One man threw a chair at Wriley, but he dodged it. Then, another one launched himself at Wriley, who knocked him out with his elbow.

"How is your little nun?" Darel provoked him from behind the bar.

"If you guys have the gut, come after me. Don't take it out on a woman," Wriley replied.

"That's because she is your woman," Scott said.

"Fucking bastards, how dare you lay your hands on her," Dean said as he beat up a guy.

Wriley jumped over the bar to shoot Darel, who dodged and threw a bottle of wine at Wriley but missed. As Darel scrambled away, Wriley shot him in the back of both thighs, and then Scott tackled Wriley from the back. They both dropped to the floor and started brawling.

"Wriley!" Eve called out.

Wriley looked up at her with Scott on top of him. "Eve!"

Scott used the opportunity of Wriley being distracted and sunk a jackknife into his right rib.

"Wriley!" Eve cried out.

Wriley knocked Scott to the side with a punch to the face.

Dean ran over to Eve and grabbed her arm. "Eve, you shouldn't be in here."

Eve broke away and ran over to Wriley, who was trying to get up.

"Wriley." Eve grabbed his arm.

"Eve, I told you to stay in the car," Wriley said.

"Hello, Sister, we meet again. Did you miss playing with us," Scott said as he tried to get up.

Eve looked away, afraid to face them.

"You will never touch her again," Wriley said as he grabbed a pistol from his back and pointed it at Scott.

"No, Wriley, don't." Eve shook her head and tried to stop him.

Wriley wrapped his left arm around her head to cover her eyes with his hand and turned her toward his body as he was ready to fire the shot. Eve covered her ears as the loud sound rang through her ears. Wriley fired several times at Scott, then at Darel, to make sure they would never ever touch Eve again.

Eve was shaking against his chest.

"Let's go," Wriley spoke softly in her ear as he removed his hand from her eyes.

Eve slowly gazed up at him, frightened at the person she was looking at. Eve and Wriley came out first while Dean set the place ablaze, consuming seven dead bodies.

As soon as Eve got outside, she broke free from Wriley and ran away. Wriley caught up to her and grabbed her around the waist.

"Eve," Wriley called.

"Please let me go," Eve cried out.

"Where do you want to go?" Wriley asked.

"I don't know. I just know that I can't stay with you. I don't know who you are anymore. You're not the Wriley from thirteen years ago." Eve cried.

Wriley turned her around. "Eve, there are many things you don't understand, and I can't explain them to you either. I may not be the same person, but my feelings for you have never changed."

"What is it that you do? How can you take away a person's life so easily without any hesitation?"

"Those guys hurt you. I can't let them live."

"You can't play God. It's not your job to decide who lives or dies."

"God never answers my prayers. If he knows how to run things, I wouldn't have to take matters into my own hands."

"Wriley, I'm afraid to be with you. Your hands are stained with blood."

"Eve, I'll never hurt you. You're the only person I love in this world."

Eve shook her head. "I can't have you hurt others."

"Eve, please, come back with me first."

"Yes, sis, just come with us for now. Bro is hurt. We should take care of his wound first," Dean said.

Eve looked down at Wriley's shirt, drenched with blood, then again at him. She could tell he was in pain, and he refused to let go of her. She grabbed his arm and walked him to the car.

"We should take him to the hospital," Eve suggested.

"That won't be necessary. Home is fine," Wriley said.

Dean opened the car door for them and closed it after they climbed in.

Dean and Eve helped Wriley to the bed. Wriley took off his shirt to reveal the wound, plus old scars from his rough upbringing. Eve couldn't handle the opened flesh wound and backed away.

Dean looked at her. "Sis, I need your help."

Eve shook her head. "I'm sorry, I can't." She continued to back further away.

Wriley looked at her. "That's fine. She is probably afraid of blood. Don't make her."

"All right." Dean went to get the medical kit and then handed Wriley an oxycodone/acetaminophen to take first. "I'm going to stitch you up now."

Wriley nodded his head.

"It's going to hurt, Bro."

"Just do it."

"Here goes," Dean said as he began to stitch up the wound.

Eve watched Wriley clench his teeth and fists to bear the pain. She backed up against the wall, slid down to the wooden floor, and started crying. She wanted to help him, but she was frightened of the sight.

After Dean finished, Wriley looked over at Eve.

"Eve," Wriley called to her.

"I'm sorry I couldn't help you," said Eve.

"That's all right. Dean already took care of it. I'm fine now, don't worry. You can come over now."

Eve shook her head and buried her face in her arms. Dean took one look at her, then back at Wriley, and shook his head. They both knew it was hopeless. Just when they thought Eve was getting used to living with Wriley, everything was up in the air again at the turn of today's event. Dean left them alone and went out to the living room to rest.

Wriley bore the pain and dragged himself out of bed over to Eve. He crouched down in front of her and placed his hands on her arms. "Eve, don't sit on the floor like this. It's cold." He tried to pull her up.

Eve resisted and shook her head while pushing his hands away.

"Eve, please," Wriley begged.

"I feel so confused and loss right now," said Eve.

"I know what you must be thinking," said Wriley.

"I'm terrified of you, Wriley. I don't know the man in front of me anymore."

"I'm still the man who loves you dearly, and I'll never hurt you."

"And that's what I'm afraid of. I'm afraid your love for me will cost others their lives. Even though I didn't kill them myself, I'm just as responsible."

"No, Eve. Your hands are clean in all of these." He touched her hands, but she pulled away. "I'll bear all the responsibility. It has nothing to do with you."

"Oh, Wriley, what kind of man have you become? I want the Wriley I know back," Eve sobbed with her face buried in her hands.

"Eve." Wriley wanted so badly to hug her.

Eve shook her head as she continued to cry.

"I know I'm not a good person, but all I want is to be with you and keep you safe. My world will collapse if I don't have you."

Eve couldn't say anything as Wriley continued to stare at her.

*****

Dike hastily entered the room where Seth was chilling on his couch, smoking his cigar. "Sir, the bar got burnt down," Dike reported.

"What?" Seth stood up.

"Seven of our men are dead, including Scott and Darel."

"Who the fuck did it?"

"It's probably Eli and Dean. Scott and Darel messed with Eli's girl, so he must be getting even."

"Eli. I swear I'm going to kill this guy one of these

days. He is all Javier has. Without Eli, Javier can't do shit. I can let Javier live a little longer, but Eli must go."

*****

As the pain medicine wore off late at night, Eve could hear Wriley start to moan. Eve woke up from her sleep and looked at Wriley writhing in bed. Eve got up and walked over to the bedside.

"Wriley?" She called softly.

He didn't answer her, but she could read the pain from his facial expression. She gently lifted the blanket to see the gauze soaked with blood. Eve knew she had to get Dean, so she walked toward the door and carefully opened it. She poked her head outside and saw the light was off and Dean was asleep. She felt bad waking him, so she closed the door after a moment of contemplation and walked back to Wriley.

Wriley was running a fever with sweats bubbling up from his pores. Eve opened the bottle of medicine and took out a pill. She gently placed it into Wriley's mouth and lifted his head to take a drink.

"Drink, Wriley."

Although asleep, Wriley followed the instructions and took a big gulp. Eve laid his head back down and then looked at the gauze. After some hesitation, Eve finally worked up the courage to remove the gauze and redress the wound. Wriley opened up his eyes slightly only to close them again.

Afterward, Eve went to the bathroom and wetted a small towel. She returned to Wriley's side and started wiping away the sweat. She noticed his other scars and ran her finger on one of them across his chest. She can't imagine the hardship he has endured all these years while she lived peacefully in the church's orphanage. She started to feel like she was the lucky one and that it was right for him not to take her away sooner. He probably didn't want her to suffer like he did, which made her all the more curious about what exactly he does for a living.

In the morning, Wriley opened his eyes to find Eve lying on top of the blanket next to him, with one hand holding his. He stared at her, not daring to move for fear he may wake her up.

Dean entered the room and walked up to Wriley quietly. Wriley opened his eyes to look at Dean.

"Bro," Dean spoke softly, but Wriley signaled him to be quiet with a finger to his mouth as he looked down at Eve.

Dean looked around. He saw the towel folded across Wriley's forehead and knew it was probably Eve's doing. He also noticed the bloody gauze in the trashcan and lifted the blanket to see if a fresh one had replaced it. Dean inquired about the gauze by pointing his finger at it. Wriley made a gesture with his head, indicating Eve. Dean nodded, smiled, and gave a thumbs-up before leaving the room. Wriley lifted the blanket off of him to cover Eve and closed his eyes to rest some more until Eve woke up.

Wriley's phone rang a little later, and he quickly silenced it. Eve started to stir, and Wriley looked at her. Eve slowly opened her eyes and gazed around before looking up at Wriley. She sat up when she saw him.

"You're up?" Eve asked.

"Umm," Wriley nodded.

Eve removed the towel and touched his forehead and face. “How are you feeling?”

“Much better.”

“Let me check your wound,” Eve said as she removed the gauze. “It’s not bleeding as much. That’s good.”

“Thank you for taking care of me last night.”

“Dean was asleep. I didn’t want to wake him up.”

“You’re not afraid?”

“I was, but I had no choice.”

“Next time, just get Dean. He doesn’t mind.”

“It’s all right. After doing it once, it’s not that scary anymore. Are you hungry? Let me go make you breakfast.”

“I want to take a shower first.”

“Okay,” Eve got off the bed and helped Wriley up.

Eve could barely support his weight with her shoulder as they walked toward the bathroom.

“Do you need help?” Eve asked innocently as they went inside the bathroom.

Wriley smiled and leaned in toward her face. “You want to help me shower?”

Eve embarrassingly shook her head and looked away as Wriley grinned to himself.

“I was just kidding. I’ll be fine.”

“I’ll go outside then.” Eve hurried outside, closing the door after her.

Wriley continued to grin, amused to see Eve blush.

Chapter 10
Protection

Eve walked to the kitchen and greeted Dean. "Good morning."

"Hey, good morning, sis. Is Bro up?"

"Yes, he is taking a shower. I'm going to make him breakfast."

"No need. I already made a pot of soup for him."

"Thank you, Dean. That's very kind of you to cook for us all the time."

"It's no big deal. I enjoy it. Besides, Bro saved my life, so I owe him. Here is your breakfast." Dean placed a plate on the table for Eve.

"Thank you." Eve sat down.

Dean also sat down to eat as well.

"How did you two meet?" Eve asked.

"I was a homeless teenager. He picked me up from the street and offered me a job and a place to stay. We become like brothers since."

"I see. What exactly do you guys do?"

"You mean our jobs?"

"Yes. Wriley never clearly explained it to me."

Dean could understand why Wriley wanted to keep it a secret from her, so he didn't want to ruin his effort by giving too much info. "We work for a big boss who owns a lot of properties. We help him collect the money from all the people who borrowed from him."

"Does it involve hurting people?"

Dean paused for a moment. He knew that she probably wouldn't buy it if he said no. "Once in a while, but most of the time, they are good about paying on time. Hurting them is just a last resort. We try not to touch them if it is not called for."

Eve nodded in silence, understanding a little more about Wriley's job.

"Bro is a good person. He only deals with the bad guys. He will never hurt an innocent person, and he loves you very much. He just wants to provide you with a good life."

"I know."

After Eve finished her breakfast, she returned to the bedroom with a bowl of soup for Wriley. He was sitting on the bed, trying to apply ointment to his wound.

"Let me help you," Eve said as she walked up to him and placed the bowl on the nightstand. She took the cotton tip from his hand and started dapping on his wound. "Have you taken medicine yet?"

"Yes, I just did."

"Does it hurt?"

Wriley lied and shook his head. He watched her attending to his wound with tender care. After she finished taping the gauze on, Wriley touched her hand.

"Are you still planning to leave me?"

Eve looked at him. "There's still so much I don't know about you. What other dark secrets are you hiding from me?"

"What you saw yesterday is the worst of it. I swear."

"I still can't accept the fact that you just killed a bunch of men. It goes against everything I believe in."

"I know. I know that you are like an angel, and you probably see me as some monster. You grew up in a loving and peaceful environment, while I grew up in hell. Out here, the strongest survive. If you want to keep your loved ones safe, you will have to make sacrifices, and when it comes to you, Eve, I will do whatever it takes."

"But this is not the life I wanted for us. I just want us to have a nice family and a simple life."

"I know, and I promised you would have that life. Just give me some time to sort my work out."

"You should eat the soup before it gets cold." Eve picked up the bowl of soup.

Wriley reached for the spoon.

"Here, I'll help you." Eve started to feed him.

Wriley opened up his mouth while staring into Eve's face.

Dean's phone rang. He was surprised to be receiving a call from the boss himself. "Hello, sir?"

"Dean?"

"Yes."

"I called Eli earlier, but he did not pick up."

"Oh, he must be busy."

"Did you guys ravage Seth's bar yesterday?"

Dean knew Javier had probably found out, so he couldn't lie. "Yes."

"Does this have to do with Eli's girl?"

"You know about her?"

"You guys think you can hide her forever?"

"He just wants to protect her."

"I know. I heard what they did to her. Is she okay?"

"She's fine now, but Eli got stabbed yesterday."

"How is he now?"

"He is better today, resting right now."

"I will send some men over to protect him, and his girl since Seth will not let this one go. Tell him to rest well for the next few weeks. Once he is ready to go back to work, come see me and bring the girl."

"Thanks, Boss. I'll let him know."

Javier hung up the phone.

Dean walked into the room as Wriley was finishing up the soup.

"You're done?" Dean asked.

"Yeah," Wriley said as he took a sip of the water.

"Can I have a moment with him?" Dean asked Eve.

"Of course, I will take this outside." Eve stood up and walked out.

Dean waited for the door to close before he started.

"What is it?" Wriley asked.

"Boss found out about Eve. He heard what they did to her and knew what happened yesterday," Dean reported.

"It seems like he is watching us," said Wriley.

"He is sending some bodyguards over," said Dean.

"That would be good too," Wriley commented.

"He wants you to rest for the next few weeks, and when you're ready, bring Eve to see him," said Dean.

"Since he already knows, there is no use in hiding her," Wriley added.

"You think he knows about your plan?" Dean asked.

Wriley shook his head. "I don't know. I don't think so since I haven't made any move, but Javier is clever. We have to be extra cautious."

"He loves you like a son. If you told him the truth, maybe he will support you."

"To lose his right arm? Probably not. Besides, I don't want to take that risk in case he disapproves. It will be more difficult to leave."

That night, after dressing Wriley's wound, Eve headed toward the door.

"Where are you going?" Wriley asked.

"You seem okay today, so I'm going to sleep on the sofa tonight."

"Dean is sleeping out there."

"Oh, then I will sleep on the ground."

"Just sleep on the bed." Wriley patted the bed.

Eve hesitated.

"It's big enough for two. I promise I won't touch you." Wriley grinned.

Eve quietly walked over to the opposite side and climbed into bed. She tried to stay as far from Wriley as possible. Wriley smiled as he lay down.

"Eve?"

"Hmm?" She turned to face him.

"If we are going to be a family in the future, we will have to be closer than this," Wriley smiled at her.

Eve shyly looked away.

"But, no rush." Wriley closed his eyes.

A couple of nights later, when his wound no longer hurt as much, Wriley moved closer to Eve after she fell asleep. He turned to his side and stared at her. *I'm okay with having nothing, but I must have you.*

Wriley woke to find Eve's arm across his chest. He looked at Eve, but she was still asleep. He smiled as he closed his eyes again. A little later, Eve started to move, and Wriley opened his eyes again. Eve opened her eyes and looked at him.

"I didn't dare to move in case I woke you," Wriley said.

Eve realized she had been holding him tight and pulled her arm away. "I'm sorry."

"Don't be. I'm glad you're comfortable sleeping next to me."

Eve shyly looked away and sat up.

"How are you feeling today?" Dean asked as they hung out in the living room after breakfast.

Wriley touched the spot. "Better. It's healing well."

"Does it still hurt?" Eve asked, sitting next to him.

Wriley smiled and shook his head. Even though it still hurts a little, he didn't want to worry her.

"Are you ready to take Eve to see Javier?" Dean asked.

"Who is that?" Eve asked.

"My adopted father. He wants to meet you," Wriley responded.

"I would like to meet him too," Eve said.

Wriley placed his hand on hers. "Eve, he is not a simple man. He has money and power to do things you can't possibly imagine."

Eve didn't understand entirely what he was saying, but it didn't sound good.

"Just be careful when we go to his place, and always stick by Dean or me."

"Okay." Eve nodded.

"You're scaring her. Don't worry. He is not going to do anything to you," Dean said.

"He is not only my adopted father, but he is also our boss. He dictates a lot of what I do."

"I understand," Eve said. She had an idea by now of Wriley's job. She knew Javier must be the reason why Wriley had all those scars on his body by putting him in such a line of work.

When Eve walked into the room, she saw naked Wriley coming out of the bathroom.

"Oh, sorry. I'll come back later." Eve was bashful and headed toward the door.

"It's all right, Eve. You don't have to leave or feel shy." He walked toward her. "Since we live together, you'll get used to seeing me." He spoke softly behind her right ear.

"Are you done with the bathroom?" She asked.

"Yes."

"Okay." Eve turned and walked straight to the bathroom without looking at Wriley.

He grinned as he walked over to the closet.

As Eve got into bed, Wriley made a bold move and lay next to her. Eve looked at him nervously.

"Eve, I don't want anything in this world but you."

"I'm just a simple girl."

"That's all you have to be for me to love you."

Eve gazed into his eyes.

"May I hold you?" Wriley asked.

Eve was silent for a second before nodding her head. Wriley smiled as he slid his left arm under her head and placed his right arm across her body.

"When we get away from here, we can have a small wedding ceremony if you want. For me, it doesn't matter because, in my mind, you're already my wife. My woman."

Eve slowly turned toward Wriley. "What if you get bored of me?"

"Never."

"I don't need a wedding. Just having you is enough."

They hugged each other, and just like that, they were married in spirit. There was no need for a ceremony or any witnesses. In their hearts, they already belonged to one another, and they don't have to prove it to anyone.

Wriley grinned as he held her tight. "Eve?"

"Hmm?"

"When are you ready to be intimate with me?"

Eve didn't know how to reply. "Are you tired of waiting?"

"No, I will wait as long as you need. I just wanted to check in with you."

"I don't know."

Wriley rubbed her back. "That's all right. Whenever you're ready, we can grow our family in the future. We will have a cozy home in the countryside with a nice yard to play with our kids. I can get a normal job, and we will live a peaceful life."

Eve closed her eyes and visualized the beautiful images that Wriley had painted. She smiled as she snuggled against his body.

"But in order to have kids, you can't be reserved with me as you are now," Wriley teased.

Eve didn't respond, so Wriley looked down at her.

“Eve?” Wriley whispered, but she was already asleep. He stroked her head and closed his eyes as well.

Chapter 11
Failed

A couple of weeks later, Dean drove Wriley and Eve to Javier's mansion. Eve admired the grand property as they got closer to the mansion, well secured behind a huge gate with guards surveilling the grounds.

Javier greeted them warmly in the guest room.

"You must be, Eve." Javier extended his hand to her.

"Hello." Eve shook his hand, and Javier embraced her tiny hand with his.

"I'm Eli's father."

"Yes, he has told me."

Javier looked at Wriley. "Oh, he did. That's good. How is your wound, son?"

"It's healed," Wriley answered.

"Good. So, you're the girl that Eli loves since childhood?" Javier asked.

Eve looked at Wriley shyly. Wriley has been carefully observing Javier's intentions.

"It's lovely to meet you finally. I can see why Eli falls for you," said Javier.

"It's nice meeting you as well," replied Eve.

"I have some things to discuss with Eli. Do you mind?"

Eve shook her head. "No, not at all."

"Great, please make yourself at home. Kat!" Javier called out to his housekeeper, who hurried down the hall.

"Yes, sir?"

"Get them some nice drinks and snacks, will you?"

"Yes, sir."

"Come with me," Javier said to Wriley and walked off with Ben and Jeff.

Wriley turned to Dean. "Watch Eve."

"I will," Dean assured.

Wriley followed after Javier.

"Sit," Javier said as he sat down on his sofa in his office.

Wriley sat down as Javier began to pour him a glass of wine.

"Let me see it," Javier said.

Wriley lifted his shirt to reveal the now-closed wound.

Javier nodded his head, glad to see it was healing well. "Why didn't you tell me about Eve?"

"I'm worried that the more people know about her, the less safe she will be."

"I could have sent men to protect her from the start. Then, nothing would have happened to her."

"Yes, I regret it now."

"And Seth's bar. You should have also let me know before you attack so that I can send assistants. You wouldn't have to do that dirty job yourself and get hurt. You know how it is with him and me all these years. What you did is no different than declaring war."

"I'm sorry. I will clean up this mess."

"You can't unless you wipe them all out."

"I will do that."

"Look at you. Usually, you're very rational. Why are you suddenly making all of these rash decisions on your own without discussing them with me first? It seems like you have changed ever since Eve shows up."

"It has nothing to do with her."

"It's obviously started with her."

"They were out to get me. Eve happened to be at the wrong place at the wrong time. Either way, I'll have to take them out sooner or later."

"I don't care about going to war with Seth. He is no match for me. I'm just worried about you. Especially now you have a woman you wish to protect. Promise me you won't do anything crazy on your own without running it by me first."

"I understand."

"Be careful from now on, if not for yourself, for Eve's sake. She seems like a nice girl."

"Yes."

"I will send more people over to protect you two."

"Thank you, Father."

"It's good you still remember that."

*****

Eve and Dean sat on the sofa as Eve gazed around the place. She realized now how wealthy Wriley's adopted father was and why Wriley could make so much money working for him.

Dean noticed she must be curious. "Want to walk around?"

Eve shook her head, afraid to intrude.

"Don't worry, this was once Bro's home. He grew up here, and I also lived here with him for a couple of years."

"It's a very nice place."

"If you don't feel comfortable walking around with me, I'll have Bro take you for a tour later."

"It's fine."

"I'm sure he doesn't mind."

Eve nodded.

"Sup, Dean." Diro approached them.

"Sup." They hugged it out.

"This is?" Diro asked.

"Eve, she is Eli's girl."

"Hello, Eve." Diro extended his hand out to her.

Eve rose and shook his hand.

"All right, I'll catch you later," Diro said before walking away.

"Later," Dean said.

Shortly after, Megan walked over. "So, you're the girl." Megan scanned Eve from head to toe.

"Hi, Megan." Dean dreaded the sight of her as he sensed trouble.

"Hello," Eve greeted her, clueless of who she was.

"What is so special about you? Why did Eli choose you?"

Eve looked at Dean.

"She is Javier's daughter," Dean informed.

Eve finally got it.

"Yes, I'm the one who grew up with Eli, and we were so close until you showed up in his life again," said Megan.

"That's not true," Dean clarified.

"Shut up, Dean," Megan said.

"Megan, please," Dean begged.

"I'm sorry, I didn't know you were with him," Eve said.

"She is not," Dean corrected.

"Sorry? Does it mean you will let him go?" Megan asked.

"I will let him decide," Eve said.

"I knew it. What a slut?" Megan said, suddenly slapping Eve across the cheek.

Dean grabbed Eve's arm. "Eve, are you alright?"

Megan felt a strong hand grasp on her shoulder and was turned around. Then she felt a sharp, forceful pain across her face that made her drop to the floor.

"Wriley!" Eve ran over to help Megan, but Wriley stopped her.

Wriley touched Eve's face. "Are you okay?"

"I'm fine. You shouldn't have hit her."

"You dared slap me?" Megan cried out as she tried to stand up with Dean's help.

"How dare you hurt her?" Wriley asked her back.

Megan broke away from Dean and approached them, but Dean soon held her back. "Because of that bitch you even hit me?"

"Don't insult her." Wriley took a step forward, but Eve held him back. Wriley looked at Eve, who shook her head.

"Don't. You shouldn't hit a woman," said Eve.

"I don't care if she is a woman or not. Anyone who hurts you has to pay," said Wriley.

"Don't forget that I'm your boss's daughter," Megan reminded.

"Because you're his daughter, that's why you're still standing," Wriley said.

"You're threatening to kill me?" Megan asked.

Eve shook her head at Wriley. "No."

"I won't, but if you ever lay another finger on her again, I will chop off your hand whether you are your father's daughter or not."

"You dared?" Megan said as she pointed her finger at him and charged forward.

"Stop it, Megan," Dean pleaded.

"Someone, take Megan away," Javier ordered from the balcony upstairs.

"Yes, sir," Diro said as he came from the hallway after hearing all the commotion.

He and another man hurried over to seize Megan and relieved Dean.

"Let me go." Megan struggled to break free.

"Listen to your father," Diro advised.

"Father, you're going to let him treat me like that?" Megan asked.

"Calm down, Megan. You're wrong in the first place," Javier said.

"Dad!"

"You guys can leave," Javier said to Wriley.

Wriley lifted Eve into his arms and carried her outside, with Dean following them. Eve turned back to look at Megan.

"Father, I'm your daughter. Shouldn't you be on my side?" Megan cried out.

"I'm on your side. If I didn't stop, you could get seriously injured."

"You wouldn't let him hurt me, would you?"

"You know very well the kind of person Eli is. You shouldn't have touched his woman. The people who did are no longer alive. Don't follow in their footsteps," Javier said and turned to walk away.

"Humph." Megan broke free from the two men and stormed away.

Dean apologized as they walked toward the car for failing his duty. "I'm sorry, Bro, I couldn't stop her in time."

"I gave you one task," Wriley was furious.

"I know I'm sorry. I was careless. It won't happen again."

"I'm not the one you should be apologizing to."

"I'm terribly sorry, sis."

"It's all right. I'm fine. It's not his fault. Please don't blame him," said Eve.

"Open the door," Wriley ordered.

"Yes." Dean opened the door.

Wriley placed Eve in the back seat and climbed in. He started to touch her face like she was a precious egg. "Does it hurt?"

Eve shook her head and touched his hand. "Wriley, I don't want you to keep hurting other people because of me."

"They are the ones who started it first. If I don't teach them a lesson, they will continue to hurt you."

"But you should never hurt a woman."

"I already let her live."

"Wriley."

"Forget about her. Let's get you home and place some ice on your cheek."

As they drove away, a car with four bodyguards inside followed them.

Three of them walked down the hallway toward their apartment with four guards behind them. In front of their apartments stood another two men that Javier also sent to protect them. Immediately, Eve put her hand up to cover her nose, and Wriley looked at her.

"Which one of you smoked?" Wriley asked.

"I did." Jorge raised his hand.

"Eve can't stand the smell of cigarettes," said Wriley.

"I'm sorry," Jorge apologized.

"Next time, step outside if you want to smoke," Wriley instructed.

"Yes, sir," replied Jorge.

Wriley hurried inside his apartment with Eve.

"If you boys want to take a smoke break, just do it outside my balcony. You can also take turns resting at my place," Dean offered.

"Got it," Jorge said.

"Thank you, Dean," Lucas said.

Dean entered his apartment.

Wriley walked into the bedroom, holding an ice pack wrapped in a paper towel. He sat on the bed facing Eve and placed it gently on her left cheek.

"It doesn't hurt anymore," Eve said.

"Just placed this on for a while so it won't get swollen. I hate myself for failing to protect you time after time."

"It's not your fault."

"Soon, I will take you far away from here."

"I know." After a moment of silence, Eve spoke again. "That woman must like you a lot."

"I don't like her."

"You grew up with her. Is it true you two were close before I showed up?"

"She lied to you. I was never close or interested in her, although she liked to tag along with me when we were young."

"Why don't you like her since you grew up with her much longer than you know me?"

"There can only be one woman in my heart, and you already occupy that space. I don't have room for anyone else."

"If you had never met me, would you have liked her?"

"No. I don't care for women like her, so don't feel bad."

"Wriley." Eve reached for his hand.

"Do you love me?" Wriley asked suddenly.

Eve looked into his eyes. "I do. I wouldn't have given up my vows if I didn't love you."

"In this life, I will never love another woman besides you." Wriley placed the ice pack on the bed and touched her face, pulling her closer to kiss her.

His movement was slow as he studied Eve's response. Eve showed no sign of objection, so he landed his lips on hers. The kiss was strange at first, for neither of them had the experience, but gradually, it became more profound and passionate. Wriley could no longer resist her. He slowly laid her down on the bed and took off his shirt. Then he began to pull up her shirt and helped her remove it.

Their hearts were pounding against each other as Wriley lay on top of her. Wriley stroked her head and kissed her. He ran his hand down her left side and wrapped it around her thigh, lifting it to the side and allowing her to open up to him. He failed to penetrate on the first try.

"Eve, you have to relax yourself. I can't enter if you're this tense," Wriley spoke softly.

Eve looked at him and nodded once.

Wriley attempted again and slowly slipped inside her. Eve held her breath from the sensation of him entering her body. A few seconds later, she started to relax her body as he rocked gently back and forth above her. After they reached the climax, Wriley rested on her body.

"Did I hurt you?" Wriley lifted his head to ask her. Eve shook her head slightly, and the two kissed again.

*****

Dean opened his door and carried out four plates of food. "Here you go, boys."

"Good morning, Dean. Oh wow," Ken greeted.

"Thank you, Dean," Roberto said.

"You're welcome," replied Dean.

They all enjoyed the food as they dug in.

"I have to say, Dean, if you weren't in this business, you would make it as a fine chef," Ted complimented.

"Yeah, you think so?" Dean asked.

"Certainly," replied Ted.

"Thanks," said Dean.

"Yeah, why don't you talk to Boss? Ask him to open up a restaurant for you," Cam suggested.

"You know what. I should," said Dean.

"Do it," Ken supported.

"Eli will have to find himself another bro," Roberto joked, and everyone laughed.

"I can't bear to leave him either. Maybe when we retire from this job," Dean said.

"Retired? Isn't Eli going to take over for the big boss?" Cam asked.

"Yeah, you're right." Dean quickly corrected himself before giving too much away. "Well, enjoy the food."

"Thanks again," Ted said.

"No problem." Dean entered Wriley's place.

Wriley opened his eyes and turned to look at Eve, who had her bareback toward him. Wriley turned on his side and started tracing the scars on her back. *God, why must you make her pay for my sin? If you want to collect your debts, I will gladly pay for them after this life. I will bear all of our sins. Just leave her out of this. She deserves to live a peaceful life.* He moved in to kiss her back, and Eve started to stir. She turned around to face him.

"Good morning," Wriley smiled at her.

"Good morning," Eve greeted shyly.

"I want to wake up to you like this every morning for the rest of my life," Wriley said.

Eve smiled.

"Let's have breakfast," he said.

Eve nodded in agreement.

Wriley showered first and came out to the kitchen.

"Did you two stay up late last night?" Dean asked as he placed the plates of food on the table.

"Why?" Wriley asked him back.

"Look at what time it is? It's already past ten," said Dean.

"Are you my mother? Are we not allowed to sleep in?" Wriley asked with irritation.

"Sleep in?" Dean sat down and studied Wriley's face for a brief moment. "You two did it, didn't you?" Dean teased.

"I don't know what you're talking about." Wriley tried to keep a straight face as he started eating.

"You can't hide from me, Bro. It's so obvious. You have the after-sex glow."

"Shut up and eat your breakfast." Wriley threw a sausage at Dean.

Dean laughed as he picked up the sausage and took a bite out of it. "Good for you, Bro. I'm happy for you."

Eve opened up the door and walked out. They both turned to look at her, and then Wriley briefly warned Dean. "You better not say anything that makes her uncomfortable."

Wriley stood up and helped Eve into her chair.

"Thank you." Eve sat down.

"Good morning, sis," Dean greeted.

"Good morning," Eve greeted back.

"Did you sleep well last night?" Dean asked.

Eve nodded her head.

"I'm sure you did," Dean teased, then let out a grunting sound as Wriley kicked him in the shin.

"Are you okay?" Eve looked at the two of them, confused about what was going on.

"Yeah, I accidentally bumped my leg," Dean lied with a smile, then looked at Wriley, who gave him a death stare.

*****

Wriley walked over and sat down next to Eve, putting his arm around her. She was watching TV with Dean, turned, and smiled at Wriley.

"Dean, it's getting late. You should go back to your place," Wriley suggested.

Dean looked at his watch. "Bro, it's only eight."

Wriley stared at him, and Dean received his message. "Right, it is late, and I'm also getting sleepy." Dean stood up and pretended to yawn as he stretched his arms outward. "Okay, I'm going to head out. Good night."

"Good night," Eve said.

"Night," Wriley said.

"You kids have fun. Don't stay up too late," Dean said before exiting.

Eve looked at Wriley, uncertain of what Dean was talking about.

"Sup," Dean greeted the four guards.

"Sup, Dean," they greeted him back.

"Guess what guys?" Dean whispered, smiling deviously.

"What?" Several of the guys asked at once.

"Eli finally lost his virginity," Dean said, trying not to laugh out loud.

All the guys started laughing.

"Sshhh…" Dean gestured for them to quiet down so Wriley wouldn't find out.

"You mean, he just got laid for the first time," Ted asked.

"Yeah," Dean nodded.

"Awe, our boy is all grown up," Cam teased.

"I don't believe it. I mean, a guy like Eli should have girls lining up to sleep with him," Ken remarked.

"There are. All the girls at the club wanted to, but the ones that were bold enough to flirt with him got fired by Megan, remember?" Dean helped them recall.

"Yeah, you're right," Ken agreed.

"Anyway, don't tell him I told. He is going to kill me," Dean warned them.

"Don't worry, brother," Roberto said.

Dean opened his door. "Good night," Dean said before entering his place.

"Good night," the men replied.

The guards had set up a small table in the hallway, playing cards to pass the time and sometimes taking turns resting at Dean's place.

Wriley picked up the remote control and turned off the TV. "Let's go to bed."

"Okay," Eve replied.

She didn't get a chance to stand when Wriley scooped her up into his arms and carried her to the bedroom. Wriley kicked the door closed with his foot and laid Eve down on the bed. She looked at him and knew what was going to happen next.

In the morning, Eve was awoken before Wriley. She gently lifted his arm off her belly to get out of bed, but Wriley pulled her closer and held her tighter with his chest against her back.

"Don't go. Stay with me a little longer," Wriley mumbled behind her neck before kissing it.

Eve closed her eyes and allowed herself to be absorbed in his embrace.

*****

"No one has figured out how to get Eli for me?" Seth asked.

"He hasn't stepped foot outside," Dike replied.

"Actually, I want his girl instead. I want to know why Eli is obsessed with this woman enough to kill my men and burn down my bar."

"Eli is very protective of her. He never let her out of his sight. We can't touch her now since Javier has sent a bunch of men to protect them," Antonio said.

"So, you are telling me I got a bunch of useless guys working for me?" Seth asked.

"No, sir," Antonio replied.

"This girl. I must get my hands on her," Seth said.

"Yes, sir, we will figure something out," Dike said.

"Why don't we come up with a way to take both Javier and Eli out?" Antonio suggested.

"You're right. Once Javier is gone, I can finally be king of New York again," Seth agreed.

*****

Wriley knew Eve was bored from staying at home all day.

"Let's go watch a movie," Wriley suggested as they were having breakfast.

"Sure," Eve nodded in agreement.

"Yeah, it's been a while since I went to a theater," Dean chimed in.

They got ready after their meals and stepped out into the hallways.

"Good morning," the guards greeted them.

"Good morning," Eve and Wriley greeted back.

"We are going to watch a movie," Dean said.

"Okay, we will follow," Jorge said.

Then suddenly, the men looked at Wriley and started clapping.

Dean freaked out, worried that they would give him away. Wriley and Eve stared at the men in confusion.

Wriley figured Dean probably said something to them about him and Eve. He gave Dean a death stare, and Dean shrugged his shoulders with an innocent smile, pretending not to know what the whole commotion was about.

"Let's go," Wriley put his arm around Eve's shoulder and nudged her along, away from this awkwardness. As they walked away, Wriley turned his head toward Dean and signaled a cut to the throat.

Dean still committed to his act with a gesture of 'I didn't say anything.'

Wriley didn't believe him, turned his head, and looked at Eve, who smiled shyly toward him.

Dean turned around and waved his hands in an X motion to the men to quit clapping. They complied and chuckled among themselves.

Dean walked on while shaking his head and knew he was in deep trouble now.

After returning from the movie, Wriley waited for Eve to enter the bedroom first before turning to Dean and grabbing his shirt.

Dean knew what was coming, pretended to look ahead, and called out, "Oh, hi sis."

Wriley, worried Eve would see him get aggressive, quickly let go of Dean's shirt and turned around to see an empty room.

Dean wittily try to dodge the confrontation but Wriley quickly grabbed his collar and pulled him back.

"Nice try," said Wriley raising his fist.

"Eve is coming," Dean said.

"I'm not going to fall for your trick again," said Wriley.

"Really, I'm not lying," Dean reaffirmed.

"Wriley? What's going on?" Eve asked.

Wriley quickly turned around and dropped his hand. "Nothing," he replied.

"Sis, you got to help me. I made a mistake earlier and Bro wants to teach me a lesson," said Dean.

Eve walked up to them and touched Wriley's arm. "Wriley, please don't hurt Dean."

Wriley gave Dean a dirty look and let go of his shirt. "I was just messing with him." Wriley tried to reassure Eve.

"Yeah, we are just playing, bye," Dean said and quickly ditched the scene.

Wriley smiled awkwardly at Eve who was still confused.

"You guys almost got me killed," Dean half-joked, half-serious with the guards.

“Sorry,” they apologized and then laughed quietly again among themselves.

Chapter 12
Ask

Dean saw a drastic change in Eve and Wriley's relationship in the following weeks. Eve was no longer hesitant to be close to Wriley, and he was no longer reserved in showing his affection for her in front of others.

They hung out in the living room after lunch. As Eve and Dean were chatting, Wriley walked over to her and handed her a glass of water.

Eve looked up at him. "Thank you," Eve said and took a sip.

Wriley sat beside her and tucked her hair behind her ear. Eve turned and smiled at him before placing the glass on the table.

Dean watched them and grinned. "Where is my water?" Dean joked.

"Get it yourself," Wriley replied as he kept his eyes on Eve and wrapped his arm around her side.

"So biased," Dean teased.

"I will get it for you." Eve was ready to get up, but Wriley pulled her back down.

"He can get it," Wriley said.

"No need, sis, I was just joking."

Then, Wriley received a call from Javier. "Hello?" Wriley answered the phone.

"We got one of Seth's men who is close to him. I will leave it up to you to find out what Seth is planning."

"Got it."

Javier hung up the phone, and so did Wriley.

Wriley looked at Eve and Dean. "I have to step out for a little bit later. Dean, you can stay here with Eve."

"You sure you don't need me to go with you?" Dean asked.

"Yeah, I'll take two men in front with me. The rest can stay behind."

Eve didn't like the sound of his mysteriousness. It can only mean he was doing something dangerous.

"Do you have to go?" Eve grabbed Wriley's arm as he was getting ready to leave.

Wriley could tell Eve was worried for him. He held her hands to comfort her. "Yes, don't worry. I'm just going to talk to someone. I'll be back in a couple of hours. Dean will be here with you, so you should be fine. Have you finished all those books?" Wriley tried to change the topic.

Eve looked at the bookshelves and shook her head.

Wriley smiled. "When you finish them, I'll get you a new set."

"It will be a while before I finish reading them."

"That's fine, take your time. I'll head out now." Wriley kissed her cheek before walking out.

*****

Seth's man was tied up in a chair surrounded by Javier's men. Wriley had his back to him, putting on the handclasp fist.

"Let's make this quick. I have someone I love waiting for me at home. Now tell me, what is Seth cooking up?" Wriley turned around to face Dike.

"I ain't telling you shit," Dike said.

Wriley gave him a good punch in the face. "We can make this fast and easy or long and bloody. I'll let you decide."

"You don't scare me. You better watch your little nun. Too bad the other guys didn't have enough time to do her. Once Seth gets his hand on her, I heard he will fuck her himself."

Wriley blood boiled at the mention of Eve. He punched Dike in the throat, and Dike started coughing up blood. Wriley grabbed his hair.

"You think I'll let anyone touch her again? I will cut off their dicks if they come anywhere within a mile of her."

Dike laughed. "Of all the women on earth, a devil-like you fell in love with a nun. Are you hoping that she would pray for all your sins?"

"You have no fucking right to comment on my life. Now tell me how Seth is planning to surprise me, or else I will slit you from head to toe."

Dike spitted out the blood at Wriley. "Fuck you!"

"Remove his clothes. I don't have the patience to play around today," Wriley ordered his men.

*****

Eve has been worrying about Wriley all afternoon. She couldn't focus on her reading because she was distracted by the fear that Wriley might get hurt like last time or, worse, not make it back at all.

Wriley returned home after he obtained all the information he needed. As soon as he stepped foot inside,

Eve popped up from the sofa and pranced over to him. She was glad to saw him safe.

"You're back," Eve said with relief, and she hugged him tight.

Wriley smiled at her excitement to see him as he embraced her back. "Yes." He touched her face with his left hand.

"She was anxious all afternoon," Dean reported.

Eve shyly looked down and noticed Wriley's fist was red and scratched up. "Your hand."

"It's fine. It was just an accident. Don't worry. It doesn't hurt," Wriley tried to comfort Eve, but she could see through his lies while Dean had an idea what happened.

They made love again that night, getting more comfortable with the motions each time. Eve nestled in Wriley's arms afterward.

"Did you hurt someone again today?" Eve asked, dreading to hear the truth.

Wriley took in a long breath and looked at Eve. "It's better that you don't ask me about my work, and I don't want to have to lie to you either."

Eve was sad by the response, slowly turned around, and moved away. Eve knew that there was nothing she could do to change his mind, but since she had already chosen to be with him, she couldn't just walk away now.

Wriley looked at her. He could sense the conflicts within her mind. He moved closer to her, placing his cheek on hers, and wrapped her with his arms. "Eve, whether I tell you the truth or not, it'll still make you uneasy, so it's better that you don't know the details. Besides, you're too pure. I don't want to contaminate you with the things going on in my world. You wouldn't be able to handle it with your pure mind. I already have everything planned. It won't be long before we leave this place."

Eve was silent for a moment. "Wriley?"

"Yes?"

"I want to look for my parents." When Eve noticed Wriley was quiet, she turned around to face him.

"Why do you want to find them?" Wriley finally asked, worrying that she was planning to leave him.

"I just want to know who they are."

"And then what?"

"I don't know."

"Eve, if they wanted to see you again, they would have come looking for you in the past twenty-five years of your life, but they didn't."

"Maybe they have some hardships like you did."

"I doubt they shared the same problems that I had. The difference is I've always planned to come back for you, and I did. If you search for them now, they may not want to see you."

"If they really don't want to see me, that's fine, but I want to try at least to reach out to them."

Wriley laid on his back with the back of his left hand resting on his forehead and sighed. "Eve, it's not that I don't want you to reunite with your family, but I just don't want you to get hurt. Plus, we are going to move away soon. What's the point of seeing them now?"

"I know we will be leaving this place soon. That's why this is my last chance to see them."

"What if they are bad people?"

"I know you have met a shared number of people like that, but not everyone in the world is bad."

"What if they want to keep you close to them? Then does that mean we have to be separated again?" Wriley was worried that he might lose Eve.

Eve touched his face and assured him. "No, I'll never leave you. I just want to know if they are alive and well. Perhaps also listen to their reasons why they gave me up. But no matter what happens, I'm your wife now. Nothing can separate us. If I don't try, I'm afraid I may regret it for the rest of my life, wondering if they wanted to see me just as much."

Wriley touched her hand. "If you really wish to find them, I'll help you."

"Thank you."

"I can't guarantee that we would find them or if they are willing to come forward."

"That's fine. I understand."

*****

Wriley asked Dean to help post a message through a news channel.

Thanh Ton was serving the customers in the restaurant and paused when she heard the news.

"An Asian-American New Yorker woman is in search of her parents who gave her up almost twenty-five years ago and left her at St. Mary Church's doorstep on Christmas Eve. If you are the parents or happen to know who the parents are, please get in touch with us via the information provided below," the female news anchor announced.

Under the screen were the phone numbers and emails of the news station.

"We wish her the best in reuniting with her family," the male anchor added.

"Yes, absolutely," the female anchor agreed.

Thanh Ton quickly grabbed a pen and wrote down the numbers. She spent that night staring at the piece of paper with the contact information, contemplating whether she should call them.

The following day, during her break, Thanh went out to the back alley and decided to make the call.

"Hello. I saw the message yesterday about a woman searching for her birth parents. I believe I'm the person she is looking for her."

Wriley, Eve, and Dean were hanging out in the living room when Dean received a call.

"Hello?" Dean answered. "That's great. They found your mother," Dean said to Eve.

Eve couldn't believe it as she looked at Wriley, and he smiled at her. Wriley wrapped his arm around Eve as they listened.

"Yes, please give me her phone number, and we will contact her," Dean continued as he grabbed a pen and paper from a nearby drawer. He scribbled down the name and number. "Thank you very much." Dean hung up the phone and walked over to them, handing them the piece of paper. "The lady who claimed to be your mother is Thanh Ton, and here is her phone number."

Wriley reached for the paper. "Thanks."

"Yes, thank you, Dean," Eve said.

"I just did as Bro instructed. I'm glad someone was willing to reach out."

Wriley called Thanh, who still lived in New York, and arranged for both sides to meet up. Eve was too excited to sleep the night before.

Eve turned to her side, facing Wriley. He opened up his eyes and touched her face.

"Can't fall asleep?" He asked.

"I'm excited but also nervous about tomorrow. What if she is mad at me for trying to find her?"

"Eve, you're overthinking things. Of course, she is not mad at you. Otherwise, she wouldn't have reached out."

"You're right. But what if she is not my mother?"

"Well, what is the chance of another woman dropping her baby girl off at St. Mary Church's steps twenty-five years ago on Christmas Eve?"

"That's true."

Wriley smiled. "Eve, everything is going to be okay. If you don't sleep now, you may not have the energy to chat with her tomorrow."

Eve nodded her head and closed her eyes. Wriley put his arm under her head and hugged her.

They arrived at the park where Thanh and her son, Jay, waited. Wriley held Eve's hand as she nervously walked up to her mother. Eve and Thanh were emotional when they saw each other, and no doubt they were mother and daughter because of their strong resemblance. Thanh walked toward Eve as she stared at her daughter's face, which she hadn't seen for twenty-five years and thought she would never see again.

"Hello," Eve greeted her.

"Hello," Thanh greeted back. Both felt shy and awkward.

"I'm Eve," Eve introduced herself.

"Eve?" Thanh wondered if her name was a pure coincidence.

"Yes. You dropped me off on Christmas Eve, so Mother Mary decided to name me Eve."

"I see. It's quite a lovely name," Thanh commented.

"And this is my husband, Wriley," Eve introduced.

Wriley smiled at the word husband. "Hello." Wriley shook Thanh's and Jay's hands.

"Hi," Jay greeted.

"Hello. I'm happy that you're married," Thanh said.

"And this is Dean, our friend," Eve introduced.

"Hello." Dean shook Thanh's and Jay's hands.

"Hi," Jay greeted.

"This is your half-brother, Jay. He is in his first year of college," Thanh introduced.

"Hello," Eve greeted and shook his hand.

"Hello, sister," Jay greeted.

"I'm sure you probably have a lot to say to each other, so Dean and I'll hang out over there," Wriley said.

"Okay," Eve said.

"I'll join you," Jay said.

"Sure," Wriley replied.

The three men walked away as Eve and Thanh sat down at a nearby bench.

"Is that your car?" Jay asked, pointing to a black Cadillac Escalade SUV.

"Yes," Wriley replied.

"Nice. You must have money."

Wriley and Dean looked at each other. They didn't like the sound of it.

"I'm glad my sister married well," Jay commented.

"My Bro takes good care of your sister, so you don't have to worry," Dean stated.

"That's good."

*****

"I'm sure you must have a lot of questions for me. I just want to start by telling you that I never stopped feeling guilty about giving you up. When I was fifteen, I went on a camping trip with my friends and I met your father there. After that camping trip, I never saw him again and found out I was pregnant. I knew my conservative parents would never accept it, so I carefully hid the pregnancy from them and gave birth to you in my car on Christmas Eve. I thought of dropping you off at the hospital, but I noticed the church's orphanage on my way there. I knew if I took you to the hospital, they would end up sending you to a foster home, so I figured it would be a safer environment for you to grow up in the church. I've missed you ever since, wondering what kind of woman you grew up to be and whether you will ever forgive me."

"Why didn't you come back to the church to look for me?" Eve asked.

"I was hoping I could return to take you home one day, but my life hasn't been the best. I never finished college, got married early, and gave birth to your brother. Then, after his father found out that I was pregnant once and gave my baby away as a teenager, he divorced me, and I had to raise my son alone. I have worked as a waitress since and struggle to make ends meet while ensuring I get your brother to college. That's why I never came back; I didn't want you to live that kind of life like us. I was hoping you are somewhere better off than we are, and it seems like you are. Your husband seems like a good man."

"He is. I'm sorry that your marriage didn't work out and that you had a difficult life. I never blamed or hated you. I knew you must have your reasons, and I'm glad you left me at the church instead of somewhere else. I had a good life growing up there. Mother Mary and the rest of the sisters took good care of me. That was also where I met my husband. His mother dropped him off when he was nine."

"I see. That's nice that you both could accompany each other."

"Yes, but part of me always wanted to find my real parents."

"And I'm glad you did. When I saw you were looking for me, I knew I couldn't keep hiding from you."

"Thank you for agreeing to meet me."

"No, thank you for not hating me." Thanh hugged Eve, and the two cried in each other arms.

After an hour of chatting, they regrouped.

"It was so good to meet all of you," Thanh commented.

"Same here," Eve agreed.

"I'm happy that you two can be reunited. If you want to see Eve again, just let me know. You have my number. I want to mention that Eve and I plan to move in the near future," Wriley said.

"Oh, where are you going?" Thanh asked.

"Not sure yet. We are still looking for a good place to settle down, but it will be far from New York."

"I see. Well, could we still talk on the phone sometimes?" Thanh asked.

Eve looked at Wriley, who nodded. "That should be fine," Wriley replied.

"Take care, Mother." Eve hugged Thanh.

"You too."

"Goodbye, sister." Jay hugged her.

"Goodbye."

"Bye," Wriley and Dean waved to them.

Wriley held Eve's hand as they walked away. "Are you happy?"

"Yes." Eve nodded.

"Good. Your mother seems nice." He didn't want to tell her that he didn't feel the same about her half-brother.

*****

"Where the hell is Dike anyway?" Seth asked his men.

"I don't know. I haven't seen him the past few days," Antonio replied.

"Has anyone called him?"

"Yes, sir. I called and texted him, but he hasn't responded at all," Lupe replied.

"Are you telling me one of my close men went MIA, and no one knows anything?"

"Do you think it's Eli's doing?" Lupe asked.

"Must be him," Antonio suggested.

"This Eli again. I must fucking kill him. Send men to keep a close watch on Eli. He must have a weakness we can use to draw him out," Seth said.

"I'm sure he does. We have to be a little patient," Antonio said.

Chapter 13
Gamble

A day after reuniting with her mother, Eve's brother called Wriley.

"Hello?" Wriley answered.

"Hi, could I speak to my sister?" Jay asked.

Wriley could sense that it was nothing good when Jay called. "Is something the matter?"

"No, I just wanted to ask my sister something really quick."

"Hold on." Wriley handed Eve the phone. "Jay is on the phone."

Eve took the phone. "Hello?"

"Hi, sister. First off, I want to say that I'm so happy to know that I have a sister."

"Oh, thank you. It's nice to have a brother as well."

"As Mom mentioned yesterday, I'm in college now, and she may be too embarrassed to tell you that we are struggling financially. I was hoping you could help us out. We don't have enough to pay for my tuition this coming semester."

Eve stood up from the sofa and walked to a distance to avoid Wriley's ears. He has been listening to her, wondering what Jay was up to.

"I'm sorry, Jay. I would love to help, but I actually don't have any money of my own. I never worked," Eve replied.

"Oh. How about your husband? He seems rich."

Eve looked at Wriley and turned away, hesitating to ask Wriley for help. "I can't just ask him—"

"Don't worry, tell him we will pay him back."

"I—" Eve hesitated.

Wriley walked over and grabbed the phone. "How much do you need?"

"Oh, brother-in-law. Uhm, I need ten grand."

"For what?"

"College tuition, and I'll pay you back in the future."

"No need. I'll bring the money to your mother so she can pay for your tuition."

"No, don't give it to my mother. I mean, she would be mad if she knew I asked for help."

"It's fine. Just tell her we insisted. I'll have Dean bring it over to your place."

"Okay, thank you, brother-in-law."

"Is there anything else you need?"

"Nope, that's it. Tell my sister I said bye."

"I will." Wriley hung up the phone.

"Wriley," Eve started.

"It's fine. That amount is nothing to me."

"I know, but you have been saving it."

"I can still afford to help your family."

"Thank you for helping them." Eve hugged him.

"Eve?"

"Hmm?"

"I don't want to hurt your feelings, but I should tell you that I don't feel good about Jay."

Eve looked at him. "What do you mean?"

"I'm afraid he will take advantage of you."

"He just needs tuition money, and he said he will pay it back."

Wriley shook his head. "No, Eve. You haven't lived in the outside world for long. You don't understand people as I do. It's not that simple with him."

"I'm sorry that my family has to bother you with money. I'll get a job. That way, I can help them without troubling you."

"Eve, you're not getting what I'm trying to say. If they truly need help, I don't mind helping them. I'm just afraid your brother has ill intentions." Wriley hugged Eve again and stroked her head. "Just know that everything I do is to protect you, and when I sense that something is off, I will have to be extra cautious."

"I know." Eve still couldn't believe that her brother would potentially harm her. She thought Wriley might just be paranoid due to the exposure of his job.

Dean delivered the money to Thanh.

"Hello, Dean," Thanh greeted at the door.

"Hello. This is for you." Dean handed her an envelope of cash.

"What is this?" Thanh asked.

"Eve and Eli heard that you are struggling to pay for Jay's tuition, so they offered some help," said Dean.

"Did Jay call them?" Thanh asked.

"Yes," Dean replied.

"That boy. I can't believe he dares to ask them for money," said Thanh with frustration.

"It's nothing. They don't mind," said Dean.

"I can't accept their money," said Thanh.

"Please do. Otherwise, you will waste their kind intention."

"All right. I'll be sure to pay them back."

"Bro, intent to give it to you."

"Please thank them on my behalf."

"I will."

"I will make sure that this money goes to Jay's education, and I truly appreciate their help."

"Okay, I'll relay the message to them."

"Thank you, Dean."

"Have a nice evening."

"You too."

"The following evening, Wriley received a call from Thanh.

"Hello?" Wriley answered.

"Hi, Wriley. Is Eve there? I need to talk to you both."

"Yes, she is here." Wriley turned on the speaker. "Your mother," Wriley said.

"Mother?" Eve asked.

"Yes. I appreciate you both for helping Jay. I never wanted to ask you for money, and I couldn't believe that Jay bothered you. We are not well off, but I can manage to put him through school. I have to say Jay has a problem with gambling. He took the money that Dean had brought over yesterday. I'm afraid he may gamble it all away."

Eve looked at Wriley.

"Where does he usually go to gamble?" Wriley asked.

"The Golden Casino," Thanh informed.

"I know that place. I'll go get him if he is there," said Wriley.

"I'll meet you there then," said Thanh.

"Okay," Wriley said and hung up the phone.

"I'll go with you," Eve said.

"Eve, it's not a good place for you to go to. Stay here, and I will ask Dean to come over."

"Please, take me with you. Jay is my brother. It would help if I were there. He may listen to me."

"All right."

Dean drove them to the casino with two guards following in a separate car.

"Of all places to go to," Dean said in the car.

Eve didn't understand what he meant, but Wriley did.

"Javier owns this casino," Wriley filled her in.

"Oh," Eve commented. She heard he owned a lot of properties. She didn't realize how big his business was.

They parked right in front of the place and got out. Because the securities were familiar with them, they could park there.

"Eve." Thanh walked up to them.

"Mother." Eve held her hands.

"I'm so sorry," said Thanh.

"It's all right," said Eve.

"Eve, you should stay out here with Dean. Inside is wreaked with smoke. I can go get him," Wriley said.

"Okay."

"I'll go with you," Thanh added, and Wriley nodded.

Wriley headed inside with Thanh and started looking around. They found Jay gambling at one of the craps tables. Wriley grabbed Jay by the back of his neck and startled him.

"What the—" Jay turned around. "Oh, it's you, brother and Mom. What are you doing here?"

Everyone stared at them.

"I'm not your brother. Where's the ten grand?"

"Jay, please give him back the money," Thanh said.

"You don't have to give it back to me, but you need to hand it over to your mother."

"I owed them money, so I had to pay them back. I had one grand left, and after gambling, I only have two hundred," Jay explained.

Wriley turned to the staff and asked, "Where is his money?"

"Here." The staff held up the envelope. Every staff member there knew Wriley, the owner's son.

"Give him back the money," Wriley demanded.

"But—" the staff hesitated.

"I said give him the money," Wriley ordered.

"Okay." The staff handed the envelope over.

"And he is underage. Why didn't you check his ID." Wriley quickly grabbed the money.

"Sorry, he looks old enough, but we will be sure to check it from now on," the staff replied.

"Here, make sure he doesn't get his hands on it again." Wriley handed the envelope over to Thanh.

"You should take it back." Thanh handed it back to Wriley.

"No, I want you to keep it. Just make sure it is put to good use."

"I'll pay you back," Thanh said.

"No need."

"Thank you."

"How nice of you. Wait, who are you exactly? Why did that guy just hand you the money?" Jay was curious.

"You don't need to know," replied Wriley.

"You work here?" Jay asked.

"Stop asking and come outside with me." Wriley dragged Jay away.

"Hey!" Jay called out.

"I forbid you from taking your mother's money or gambling again," Wriley ordered.

"You can't stop me from gambling. As long as I don't use your money."

"Jay," Thanh said.

"I don't care who money it is. You are wasting your mother's hard effort in raising you. You should focus on your education."

"Screw you. Who gives you the right to tell me what to do?" Said Jay.

"Stop it, Jay," said Thanh.

"It doesn't matter who I am. You are hurting people who care for you, including Eve, and I will not allow that."

"So, you don't care about me. You just don't want it to affect Eve."

"That's right."

Eve rushed over to them as they exited the building.

"Your husband is bullying me," Jay tattled to Eve.

"Wriley." Eve grabbed his arm.

"I'm doing this for his good," Wriley said.

"Let go of me." Jay struggled.

Wriley turned Jay around to face the securities. "Make sure he never enters this place again."

"Yes, sir," the two securities replied.

"Take a picture of his face, ID him so we will have it in the system."

"Okay," one security took out his phone and captured the image of Jay.

"Hey, you can't do that," Jay complained.

"And send his picture to all the casinos in New York. Put a notice on his record that way he can never step foot in any casinos in New York," Wriley ordered.

"Got it," the first security said.

"Fuck you!" Jay broke free and punched Wriley in the face.

"Wriley." Eve touched his face.

"Jay, no!" Thanh rushed over to stop him.

Dean quickly grabbed Jay and kicked him in the stomach. Jay flew a few feet back.

"Jay!" Thanh approached him simultaneously as their two guards grabbed Jay and pulled him up.

"How dare you hit him? You are messing with the wrong person, kid," Dean walked toward Jay, ready to throw a punch.

"Let me go!" Jay shouted.

"Please don't hurt him," Thanh pleaded.

"Dean, please," Eve called out to him, and Dean turned to look at her.

Wriley also lost his temper and stepped forward, but Eve held him back. "Wriley, no." Eve shook her head.

"If I don't teach him a lesson, he'll never learn," said Wriley.

"I beg you, please don't hurt my brother," Eve pleaded.

"He is just your half-brother," said Wriley.

"He is still my brother. Can you let him go this time?" Eve begged.

"Yes, please. I'll make sure he never causes any trouble again," Thanh promised.

Wriley looked at Thanh and Eve. "Take him home and make sure I never see his face again. I can't guarantee he'll still be alive after seeing him."

"Yes, yes, I'll take him home. I'm so sorry for troubling you," Thanh said with embarrassment.

"Tell me who you are," Jay demanded.

"Mother," Eve said.

"I'm truly sorry, Eve," Thanh apologized.

"Take them to their car," Wriley ordered his guards.

"Yes," Lucas and Jorge replied.

"Fuck you!" Jay shouted

"Shut your mouth," Thanh yelled at him.

"Jay, please," Eve begged.

"You guys can go back on your own afterward," Dean instructed the guards.

"Okay," Lucas and Jorge replied again.

"I hate you!" Jay shouted as he was pulled away.

"Be quiet. You have caused enough trouble!" Thanh followed behind.

"Let's go," Wriley said, and they climbed back into the car.

Eve touched his face again. "Wriley—"

"I told you not to search for your family," Wriley interjected, trying hard not to raise his voice at Eve. He was angry but never enough to take it out on Eve.

"I'm sorry," Eve said solemnly.

"Your brother is not a good person. You barely reunited with your family, and already he is causing problems for us. Remember that even though she is your mother, she hasn't lived with you for a single day. Her love for her son will be more than her love for you. They didn't want you in the first place."

"Bro," Dean interjected. Usually, he tried to stay out of their business, but he felt bad for Eve.

Eve kept quiet as tears fell from her eyes. Wriley looked at her and couldn't bear it. He reached out to hug. "I'm sorry, Eve. I didn't mean to make you cry."

Eve hugged him back. "It's my fault."

"No, it's Jay's fault. You don't have to take responsibility for him."

"He is still my family and has caused trouble for you."

"It's not about me. Eve, don't you get it? I just don't want it to affect you. I'm upset for you."

"I understand."

"I shouldn't blame you for wanting to find your birth parents. I just hate that it causes you to worry for them. Know that in this world, no one loves you more than I do."

As they got ready for bed, Wriley checked the bruise on his face in the bathroom mirror.

"Does it hurt? Want me to get the ice pack?" Eve asked as she walked up to him.

Wriley shook his head. "No, it doesn't hurt, but my pride is. No one has ever gotten away with hurting me without receiving something worse in return."

"I'm sorry, Wriley. I know you tried your best to hold back because of me, and I truly appreciate it. You can hit me if it makes you feel better. I'll take it for Jay."

Wriley smiled as he touched her face and pulled back a strand of hair. "No, Eve, you're the last person in this world

I would hurt. I'd rather die than inflict any sort of pain on you, and I will not forgive anyone who does either."

Eve was touched by his words, wrapped her arms around his neck, and tiptoed to kiss his bruised cheek. Wriley looked at her and then leaned in to kiss her. He hugged her off the ground and walked into the bedroom as they continued kissing.

Thanh called Wriley the next day.

"Hello?" Wriley answered.

"Wriley, I'm terribly sorry for what happened yesterday. I just don't know how to face you two anymore after that," Thanh said.

"It's not your fault."

"I'm still his mother and should take responsibility for it."

"It's over now, so don't worry about it."

"Thank you for being so forgiving. May I speak to Eve?"

"Yes." Wriley handed Eve the phone.

"Hello, Mother?" Eve asked as she rose from the sofa and stepped away.

"Eve, I'm so embarrassed to face you."

"You don't have to feel bad."

"I was so happy to be able to meet you again after all these years. I never thought I would end up causing trouble for you and your husband. I just don't know what to say other than I'm truly sorry. I hate to say this, but I feel that it is best we don't see each other again. Not that I don't want to see you. I just can't risk Jay disturbing you again. As your mother, I have failed you once. I have no right to fail you again. Please know that I'll always love you. Once Jay is older and more mature, I hope we can meet again."

"I understand."

"Goodbye, Eve."

"Goodbye, Mother."

Eve started to cry as Wriley walked over to her.

"What's wrong?"

"My mother said she will not be seeing me again because she doesn't want Jay to bother us anymore."

Wriley hugged Eve and stroked her hair. "I'm sorry, Eve. You still have me and will always have me. We both came from broken families, and two halves make a whole. You and I don't need anyone else. Just each other is enough. I'll forever love you and never abandon you. You may not matter that much to them, but you matter a lot to me. You are my world, my life, my everything. No one will cherish you more than I do."

Eve nodded and held him tight.

Wriley continued to comfort Eve as they got into bed, tapping gently on her back as they faced each other. Eve was lying on her stomach. He consoled her like putting a baby to sleep. Wriley felt sorry for Eve, but part of him was glad that he could keep her all to himself. He knew Eve's simple wish was to be wanted, and he was the only person who offered that kind of affection to her.

"When we move away, I want to get a job. I know you said I don't have to, but I don't want to stay at home all day."

Wriley nodded. "Okay, once we leave this place, you can work. What do you want to do?"

"I'm not sure."

"Since you like flowers so much, why don't I open up a flower shop for you? That way, you are surrounded by beautiful flowers every day."

Eve visualized being in a shop full of flowers that give off various fragrances. Eve nodded. "That sounds lovely." Eve smiled and closed her eyes. "I love you, Wriley."

Wriley grinned. "I love you, Eve." He kissed her forehead and watched her sleep for a while before resting himself.

Chapter 14
Rescue

Wriley finally met up with Javier to discuss the details he found out from Dike. They came up with a plan to take Seth down for good, but Wriley left out his personal agenda.

"That's what I learned from Seth's man," Wriley reported.

"Seth, you dare think about getting rid of me. Good for you. Well, we'll have to disappoint him, won't we," Javier asked.

"That is a must," Wriley added.

"Who was the kid that caused a ruckus at the casino the other day?"

"Just some reckless guy. I already took care of him," Wriley replied.

"He did that to you?" Javier indicated Wriley's bruised.

"I was distracted."

Javier sighed. "Eli, you must be more careful and not let some teenager mess with you like that."

"It won't happen again."

"Are you planning to marry Eve after we settle, Seth?"

"Yes, I've always wanted to give her a family life that she dreams of."

"I'm sure you will. I'll throw a nice wedding for you two."

"I want to offer her a quiet and peaceful life, away from all this chaos."

Javier understood where Wriley was going. "That's fine as well. In the future, you can leave most of the work to other people. I'll try not to bug you too much."

Wriley was hoping that Javier would let him go completely. "Thanks for your support."

"Of course. So how should we deal with Seth?"

*****

As soon as Jay came out of his house, he got dragged away by two men.

"Hey, who the fuck are you guys?" Jay shouted.

They were chilling in the living room in the evening when Wriley received a call from Jay.

"What do you want?" Wriley answered the call.

"Bro, I need your help," Jay begged.

Wriley turned away from Eve, who was watching him. "I'm not your bro, and I'm not going to bail you out of your mess again."

"No, no. This time, it's not my fault. Some of your friends came looking for me, and they got me tied up now."

"Friends?"

"Hello, Eli," Antonio greeted.

"Who the hell are you?" Wriley asked.

"Friends of the men you recently killed."

Wriley rose from his chair, walked swiftly into the bedroom, and closed the door.

Eve and Dean looked at each other, not knowing what was happening.

"What do you want?" Wriley asked.

"We heard you're related to this kid," Antonio replied.

"I'm not," Wriley replied coldly.

"His wife is. I'm her brother. Tell them that I'm Eve's brother," Jay jumped in.

"Oh, he is your wife's brother," Antonio said.

"We have dissociated from him," Wriley replied.

"So, you're not going to come to rescue him?" Antonio asked.

"No, you guys can do whatever you want with him," replied Wriley.

"No, wait! They got me because of you. I don't know these people," Jay yelled out.

"You don't care, but how would your wife feel if she learned that you let her brother die?" Antonio asked.

"What exactly do you want?" Wriley asked.

"I want you to come to meet us tomorrow and bring your little wife with you," said Antonio.

"I can come alone. Why do you need me to bring her?" Wriley asked.

"Oh, because we have heard so much about her. We want to meet her," replied Antonio.

"You think I'm fucking crazy? Why would I risk putting her in danger?" Wriley asked.

"If we don't see her, we will kill her brother," Replied Antonio.

"No, please. Don't let them kill me!" Jay pleaded.

"You dare drag Eve into this. I'm going to fucking kill you myself when I see you," Wriley directed it toward Jay.

"Hey, this has nothing to do with me. I don't know what beef you have with these men, but they are very pissed. I'm the victim here. Just save me. I promise I'll focus on my school from now on. I'll be a good kid and help my mother out. I'll never gamble again. Please, I'm too young to die. You gotta save me. You know Eve would," Jay cried.

Wriley had his fist to his mouth, contemplating what to do. He was stuck between a rock and a hard place. He knew that Seth's men got Jay because of him, so he was responsible for saving Jay, but he couldn't risk Eve's safety.

"Hello? Are you still there?" Antonio asked.

"Text me the time and place. I'll be there," Wriley finally replied.

"And your nun?"

"Wait, who is the nun?" Jay asked.

"Your sister, dumbass?" Antonio replied.

"She is not anymore, so stop calling her that," Wriley added.

"But she used to be. Anyway, just bring her," Antonio demanded.

"I'll bring her," Said Wriley.

Antonio laughed. "Good. Just you two and no one else. We'll have a party tomorrow."

Wriley hung up and threw the phone on the bed. "Fuck!" he screamed and started punching the bed.

It frightened Eve, and she stood up along with Dean. They headed over to the bedroom, and Dean knocked on the door.

"Bro, what's wrong?"

Wriley didn't answer as he was still enraged and struggled with what to do. He kept punching the bed.

Eve slowly opened the door. “Wriley.” Eve ran over to grab his arm.

Wriley stopped and looked at her.

“What happened? Is Jay in trouble again?” Eve asked.

Wriley hugged her.

“Wriley, please tell me. You’re scaring me.” Eve was worried sick about him and Jay.

Wriley cupped her face as he stared into her eyes. “Seth’s men got Jay and threatened to kill him if I don’t show up tomorrow.”

Eve gasped.

“Why is that kid keep getting himself into fucking trouble?” Dean asked.

“It’s not his fault this time. Seth is out to get me. They expect me to bring Eve along as well.”

“What?” Dean asked.

“They will kill him if they don’t see Eve.”

“Bro, that is clearly a trap.”

“I know, but I don’t know what fucking else to do.”

Eve was also scared, but she knew she couldn’t let her brother die. “I’ll go. If that is what they want.”

Wriley grabbed her arms. “Eve, they are actually just using Jay to get you. You are the person they want because they know that you’re my weakness.”

Eve stared at him. “Jay is my brother. I can’t let him die. Especially when he has nothing to do with this.”

“Fucking Seth.” Dean cursed. “You got to tell Javier. You can’t do this alone.”

*****

Wriley called Javier and filled him in.

"He dares threaten my son?" Javier said.

"If it's me that they want, I can handle it, but they want to involve Eve. I can't let anything happen to her," Wriley said.

"Don't worry. I won't let anything happen to either of you. Just show up as they want and play their little game. We'll have backup nearby."

"No one can escape."

"No, they won't."

*****

Wriley went to bed with Eve and waited for her to fall asleep before coming outside to discuss with Dean.

"Sis is asleep?" Dean asked.

"Yeah. I knew it was a bad idea for Eve to reunite with her family." Wriley sat down on the sofa.

"You can't blame her. Who wouldn't want to know their parents?"

"I know. That's why I stopped saying anything about it because I don't want to make her feel sad like last time."

"Let me go with you two."

"No, they made it clear they only want Eve and me."

"Damn, son of bitches. What exactly do they want with Eve?"

"I don't know, but I'm fearful for her."

"Do you think they want to keep Eve as their toy?"

"When I was interrogating Dike. He said Seth wanted to get his hand on Eve. They must have figured out how important she is to me and try to use her as a weapon to get me."

"We should cut off his fucking old balls."

"If they touch Eve again, I won't let them die in peace."

"When do you want us to storm in?"

"At ten. That's all the time I'm willing to give to their bullshits."

"You should rest early. You need the energy to fight tomorrow."

"You too."

Dean nodded. "I'll head back now."

"Okay."

"Good night, Bro."

Wriley headed back into the bedroom and wrapped his arms around Eve. He kissed her head and held her.

*****

They were nervously getting ready to head out. Wriley walked over to Eve, who was anxiously sitting on the sofa. He crouched down in front of her and took her left arm.

"Eve, I want you to wear this. You may need to use it." Wriley said as he fastened an arm sheath strap around her forearm with a mini laser knife attached to it.

Eve looked at him. "I can't kill anyone."

"You won't. This is not going to kill them. It will inflict some pain, enough to distract them so you can escape."

"Wriley, I don't want to hurt people."

"Sis, if you don't hurt them, they will hurt you, Bro or Jay," Dean said.

"Hopefully, you don't have to use it, but I just want you to keep it with you just in case," Wriley added.

Eve nodded, hoping that she would never have to use it.

"Here, put on your jacket." Wriley helped her wear the strap and then jacket.

Wriley drove Eve to the location. Dean and the rest of Javier's men followed behind at a distance and parked a couple of blocks out.

Wriley held Eve's hand as they walked in. "Don't worry, Eve. I won't let anything happen to you. Just stay close to me and do as I say."

"Okay."

Two guards stood in front of the building, looking around to ensure Wriley and Eve came alone.

"Go inside," one man said.

"There they are," Lupe said as soon as he saw them enter.

Five guns immediately pointed at them while Antonio had his on Jay's temple.

"Sis," Jay called out.

"Jay," Eve said.

"I knew you would come for me," Jay said.

"Check him," Antonio ordered, and two men headed over to Wriley.

"No need. I didn't bring any weapon." Wriley lifted his shirt to show them his front and back.

"What about the girl?" Lupe asked, and the same two men approached Eve.

Eve was frightened and got closer to Wriley.

Wriley pulled Eve behind him. “Don’t touch her. She doesn’t have any.”

“Good. You know how to play this game,” Antonio said.

“We are here as you requested. Now let him go,” Wriley demanded.

“Let him go? The fun hasn’t started yet,” Lupe said.

“What the fuck do you want? I don’t have time for this shit,” said Wriley.

“Uh oh. Looks like someone doesn’t have patience,” Antonio laughed.

“Just tell me what you want and get this over with” Wriley said impatiently.

“You killed so many of our brothers, and what the hell did you do to Dike? He has been missing,” Lupe said.

“I’m not his babysitter. Why are you asking me?”

“Don’t lie, Eli. You think we are stupid. Everyone knows that no one is capable of making a person disappear beside you,” Antonio said.

Eve listened nervously. She wondered if Wriley was indeed responsible for Dike.

Wriley smirked. “Am I supposed to take that as a compliment?”

“You have no idea of the deep shit you’re in right now. Don’t act tough,” Lupe said.

“You want revenge, is that it? What I did at the bar was also revenge for what they did to her,” Wriley said.

“They let her live, but you killed seven of them in return,” Antonio said.

"What they did to her was worse than death. I would kill them over again if that is possible," Wriley responded.

"Who do you think you are? You think Javier is the king, and you're the prince of New York?" Antonio asked.

"You know damn well who runs things around here," replied Wriley.

"Stop talking with him. He is getting on my nerves. Just beat the crap out of him," Lupe suggested.

Wriley backed away with Eve still behind him.

Antonio pointed his gun at Jay again and said, "Your life for his."

"No," Eve said.

"We won't kill you, but you need to pay for what you have done. If you can take a beating without resisting, then we'll let him go when we feel like it's enough," Lupe said.

"No, Wriley." Eve shook his arm.

Wriley looked at her and back at them. "That's all you want?"

"Yes," Lupe replied.

"You're not going to hurt her?" Wriley asked.

"We won't hurt her, just you," Antonio said.

"Okay." Wriley looked at Eve again, who kept shaking her head. He smiled at her. "A few punches are not going to hurt me."

"No, don't do it," Eve begged.

Wriley touched her face. "It's going to be okay. Just stand aside." Wriley pushed her back further near the door as he let go of her hand. "It's going to be quick," Wriley whispered.

Eve knew that help was on the way, but she was worried they might not get here soon enough.

Wriley walked toward them with his arms out. “Do whatever you want.”

Antonio signaled the men with his hand, and they approached Wriley with violent punches.

“Wriley!” Eve called out.

Wriley swallowed his pain and remained stoic. “It’s okay, Eve. I’m fine.”

The five men kept up with their abuse, and Wriley finally fell to the ground. Jay watched and felt sorry for Wriley.

“Wriley,” Eve ran over to him.

“Take her away,” Antonio said, and two men grabbed her.

“No!” Eve screamed.

“Let her go!” Wriley called out.

“You’re not in a place to make demands right now,” said Lupe.

“Please don’t hurt him. I beg you, please let us go,” Eve cried.

Antonio walked over to Eve and lifted her chin. “So, you are the girl that Eli is so crazy about. You are quite pretty.”

“Don’t touch her.” Wriley headed for Eve but was held back by the other men.

“Tell you what. I can stop hurting him and let them go if you’re willing to trade places with him,” Antonio said as he walked behind Eve and sniffed her hair.

“You bastard, you said you would leave her alone,” Wriley said.

“Yeah, leave my sister alone!” Jay yelled.

"Hey, I'm not doing anything to her. I'm just offering her a deal," said Antonio.

"Eve, don't listen to him," Wriley said.

"Shut up!" Lupe punched Wriley across the face.

"Stop! What do you want me to do?" Eve asked.

"How about you strip down right now and fuck me in front of your man."

"You fucking—" Wriley wanted to break away but couldn't with a blow to the stomach.

"No, don't do it, sis. Kill me instead," Jay voiced.

Eve looked at Jay and Wriley.

Wriley shook his head. "No, Eve. It's going to be over soon. I can handle it. Don't do it."

"Well?" Antonio asked.

Lupe punched Wriley again.

"Don't! I will," Eve agreed, tears rolling down her cheeks.

"No, Eve! I'd rather suffer worst or die," Wriley cried out.

"I can't let you die." Eve looked at him and back at Antonio, then she slowly unbuttoned her shirt to stall time while praying for Dean to come in with the rest of the crew to rescue them.

"I see why you like her. She is a brave one," Antonio said.

"Yeah, more than her man," Lupe agreed, and the rest of the men started to laugh.

"I'm going to fucking kill you. All of you," Wriley threatened.

"You crazy bastards. Don't make her do this. Just fucking kill me already," Jay cried.

"Let me go." Wriley tried to fight them but kept getting hit instead. *Dean, where are you?* Wriley was getting impatient.

"Come on, sister, we ain't got all day," Antonio rushed.

Eve's hands were shaking as she continued to undo her buttons, revealing her nude bra.

"Hurry and take it off," Lupe commanded.

"Shut the fuck up!" Wriley yelled and received another blow to his cheek.

"I'll kill you, assholes!" Jay shouted.

Eve hesitated to remove her jacket when suddenly gunshots went off outside.

"What was that?" Antonio asked.

Everyone was distracted, and Wriley used the opportunity to gain the upper hand. He started attacking the men, and they immediately shot at him, but Wriley used one man's body to shield him.

Antonio had his arm locked around Eve's neck and his gun to her head.

Dean and a bunch of men came in and started shooting.

"Bro, you okay?"

"Yeah." Wriley picked up a pistol from the dead guys.

"Stop! Or else I'm going to shoot her." Antonio threatened as all the guns in the room were aiming at him.

"Get Jay," Wriley instructed Dean.

Dean and a couple of men cut Jay loose. "Take him outside," Dean told Ken and Roberto.

"Let's go," Ken said as he grabbed Jay and led him outside.

"What about my sister?" Jay asked.

"Don't worry, she'll be fine," Roberto said as they headed outside.

"Let her go," Wriley ordered Antonio.

"She is my ticket out of here. If I let her go, you guys will kill me," Antonio said.

"If you don't, I swear I will kill you on the spot."

Antonio hesitated. He knew well that Wriley was not someone to be crossed, and he was in a tight spot with little room to negotiate.

"You have lost. Just give up," Dean added.

Wriley signaled Eve to use her knife by discretely touching his arm. Eve knew what he meant but couldn't bring herself to do it, so she shook her head.

"Let me walk out of here first. Then I'll let her go." Antonio tried to make his way toward the back entrance.

"Eve." Wriley again signaled her to use the knife.

Eve finally cautiously lifted the left sleeve of her jacket and pulled out the small knife, then gave Antonio a slapdash jab in the thigh. Antonio screamed, clutched his leg, and pulled out the knife while Eve ran toward Wriley. Wriley shot Antonio's arm to lose the gun while Dean shot him in the chest, and he hit the ground.

Wriley caught Eve in his arms and took off his jacket to cover her front. "Cover your ears, and don't turn around," Wriley instructed before walking away.

Eve knew that it could only mean one thing. He was not going to let Antonio go. "Wriley, please let him go."

Wriley kept on walking.

Antonio turned on his stomach, attempting to crawl away as Wriley headed toward him. "I thought you'd let me go as long as I don't hurt her," Antonio said.

Wriley picked up the small knife from the ground and pressed one knee on Antonio's back. "What makes you think I let you live to tell the tale after what you have done to her? You know how terrified she was just now and the way you humiliated her in front of everyone. I told you I would kill every fucking one of you for dragging us here today."

"You're a fucking liar, Eli."

"I'm already giving you an easy way out. Believe me. It could be much worse. Too bad Seth didn't come here himself. I could've ended it all today."

"Go to hell!"

"See you in hell." Wriley grabbed Antonio's hair to lift his neck, then slit his throat. Afterward, he wiped the blood off the knife with Antonio's shirt and handed it to Dean. Wriley walked back to Eve's and pulled her hands down from her ears. "Let's go home."

Eve nodded her head in tears, and they all walked outside.

"Sis, I'm glad you're okay. Who the hell are you, man?" Jay asked Wriley.

"You don't need to worry about other people's business. You and your mother should get out of New York today and never come back here. I'll transfer money into her account so she can settle down in a new place," said Wriley.

"Got it. Thanks again for coming here for me," Jay replied.

"You should thank Eve," Wriley said.

"Thank you, sister."

"Be careful from now on," Eve said.

"I will. I'm a changed man after today's event," said Jay.

"Good for you," Dean praised.

"Cam and Ted, you two take Jay back to his place and help escort them to the airport," Wriley said.

"Yes, sir," Cam replied.

"Call me if something comes up," said Wriley.

"Will do," Ted replied. "Let's go."

"Goodbye, sis, and everyone." Jay waved.

"Goodbye, Jay," Eve said.

"Bye," Dean waved to him.

"I better not get another call from you," Wriley warned.

"You won't," Jay said and walked away.

Wriley helped Eve into the car, and Dean drove them home. In the car, Wriley helped her button up her shirt.

"Are you okay?" Wriley asked.

"Umm," Eve nodded. "I wasn't the one getting hurt. You should go to the urgent care."

"I'm fine—just surface injuries won't kill me." He was used to this kind of pain. "Let me take this off for you." Wriley removed her armband and threw it onto the passenger seat so Dean could take care of it. "You did great today."

Eve shook her head and cried again.

Wriley hugged her. "Everything is okay now. We are all safe."

Eve sat on the bed that night with her arms wrapped around her knees, staring at her right hand. Wriley sat down facing her.

"Eve," said Wriley.

"I hurt someone today, and he is dead because of me," said Eve.

Wriley held her hand facing up and kissed the palm. "You didn't hurt anyone. I did. You just did what you had to do to escape."

Eve shook her head. "Everything is wrong. Everything about this is so wrong."

"I know you don't want to hurt anyone, but the people I killed are bad guys. They sell drugs, hurt innocent people, and destroy many families. I just helped rid the community of their trash."

"Are you responsible for their missing friend?" Eve asked.

"I did what I had to to protect you. These men were plotting to kill Javier and me and hurt you."

"But I can't live my life like this. Always on edge, fighting to survive. What kind of lives are we living?"

Wriley pulled her into his arms and stroked her head. "I know how you feel, but I promise it will be over soon. Just hang in there. You will never have to deal with these types of nightmares again."

Eve hugged him tightly. "Wriley, please take me away from this place as soon as possible."

"I will. I will." He kissed the side of her head. "Eve, in the future, please promise me under no circumstances will you offer yourself in return for my safety."

"But I can't let them hurt you," said Eve.

"I can take it. Even if they kill me, I won't allow you to endure that kind of treatment again. Promise me."

"Okay, I promise."

"Good."

Eve touched his face. "Your body is covered in bruises."

"I'm fine." Wriley kissed her.

Chapter 15
Plan

Eve requested another visit to the church and had a private chat with Mother Mary.

"Wriley and I are now married," Eve shared.

"That's wonderful, congratulations," said Mother Mary.

"Thank you. I also found my mother," Eve shared.

"When I came across that announcement on the news, I knew right away that it was you," said Mother Mary.

"Yes, Wriley and Dean helped me put the words out there."

"That's great that you got to see your mother again."

"Yes, but it was brief. I may not have the chance to see her again."

"Oh, why is that?"

"It's complicated. My half-brother got into some trouble, which Wriley helped bail him out of, but they have to move far away in order not to disturb our lives anymore and also for their safety."

"I see. How is life for you? You look tired from when I last saw you."

"We had many ups and downs."

"You two don't get along?"

"No, not like that. A lot has happened to us. I can't tell you all the details."

"That's fine. You don't have to."

"Wriley's job put him at risk of getting hurt, and he also hurt others."

"Does he hurt you?"

Eve shook her head. "No, he has never hurt me, nor will he, but I'm not comfortable with him hurting others, especially to protect me."

"I see. If it's his job that is bothering you, have you talked to him?"

"I have, and he promised me that he plans to take me far away from that kind of world, but I feel it's not soon enough."

"Are you considering leaving him then?"

"I don't want to, but I'm not sure if I should. I love Wriley, and he also loves me with all his being. He is very tentative to me; however, I feel just as guilty whenever he harms others. Wriley had a rough life after his parents passed away. It pushed him to a corner, and he had to fight to survive, so I don't blame him for becoming the man he is today. That doesn't make it easy for me to live with such a person. Yet, if I leave him, I don't know where else to go."

"If you need a place to stay, we can make an exception and let you live here as a volunteer. I'm just worried that Wriley may not let you leave."

"He probably won't."

"Will he hurt you if you leave him?"

"No, he wouldn't, but he will come to the church to find and bring me back or do whatever it takes to keep me by his side."

"I'm sorry, my child. I thought you two could have a happy life together, not realizing how difficult it has been for you."

"I'm happy whenever I'm with Wriley. I can't ask for a better husband. I just wish he changes his ways, which I know is impossible."

"Do you want me to talk to him?"

"Please don't. I'm worried he may be upset if he finds out I shared my concerns with you."

"Don't worry, I won't give away everything you say, but I can put in a word of advice for him and see if that makes a difference."

"You can try. I guess I just have to be patient and wait for him to take care of everything before moving away."

"You know you can always talk to me about anything troubling you, and I'll help you to the best of my ability."

"Thank you, Mother."

"May God bless you, my child, for a peaceful life."

"I wonder if he is punishing me for renouncing my vows."

"No, God does not punish people for wanting to be with the person they love, even if that means giving up being religious, and you don't have to be one to enter the kingdom of heaven. Eve, you are a compassionate person. God knows your heart, and he will never judge you." Mother Mary placed her hand over Eve's.

"I feel much better talking to you."

Mother Mary smiled warmly. "I'm here whenever you need me."

Eve smiled.

When they walked out to the car, Wriley could read Eve's eyes and knew she had been crying. He figured she must have a heart-to-heart conversation with Mother Mary.

"Wriley, may I have a word with you?" Mother Mary asked.

"Yes, of course," Wriley said.

"I'll go wait in the car," Eve said.

"Mhm," Wriley nodded.

"Bye, Mother Mary." Dean waved.

"Goodbye, Dean, and take care, Eve," said Mother Mary.

"Goodbye, Mother Mary," Eve waved.

Dean opened the door for Eve to get in while Mother Mary stepped away with Wriley.

"It has come to my attention that Eve is not in the best mood like the last time I saw her," Mother Mary said.

"What has she said to you?" Wriley was curious.

"Not much, which worries me even more. I know I don't have the right to give you advice because I'm not your mother, but I just want to remind you that when you came back for Eve, you promised to do whatever it takes to make her happy. I hope that includes making a change to your life."

"I know I haven't done my best so far; instead, I have made her suffer since she started living with me, but I told her it will only be temporary. Don't worry, Mother, I'll fulfill my promise to make her the happiest woman. I just hope she trusts me and gives me more time."

"I'm comforted to hear you say that. Remember, Eve is a gentle soul; she is not like other people you meet. Therefore, it's difficult for her to accept certain ways of life in the real world."

"Yes, I understand. I've tried to shelter her from that."

"That's good."

"I wish you two the best in your marriage."

"Thank you, Mother Mary."

"Goodbye."

"Goodbye."

Mother Mary nodded, and Wriley walked away.

Eve was nervous when Wriley got into the car, worrying if Mother Mary had shared any info that would make him uncomfortable. To her relief, Wriley smiled, grabbed her hand, and kissed it.

"Thank you for remaining by my side. I know I have made you suffer a lot, and I'm grateful you haven't left me," said Wriley.

Eve rested her head on his shoulder. "What did Mother Mary say?"

"She is just concerned about your well-being and reminded me to take better care of you."

"I'm sorry I have caused her and you to worry."

"You don't have to apologize. It's my fault for not being the best husband."

"You are. It's just I wish we were somewhere else."

"I know." Wriley kissed her crown and caressed his cheek against it.

They returned home and sat on the sofa. Eve felt guilty for sharing too much info with Mother Mary.

"Are you upset that I talked to Mother Mary?" Eve asked.

Wriley wrapped his right arm around her. "No, Eve. I don't care if you tell her everything about me."

"I didn't."

"It doesn't matter. It doesn't bother me whether she knows or not. She is someone we can trust, and I know she mainly cares about your happiness. There is nothing you can do that will cause me to be upset at you."

"Wriley, you are so good to me."

"Not enough. I know things have been rough for you. Believe me; there are times I wish I hadn't walked down the path I did. Especially not after what I have put you through. If I could foresee the future, I would have chosen differently. I would have returned to the church after my parents died to be with you. We could have grown up side-by-side and left the church together. But you know we can't go back in time. I never liked my job and am not proud of the person I have become. I also don't enjoy hurting people. I hate every bit of it as much as you do. We can't undo the past. Life is what it is, and I'm struggling to do what is right by you."

"I know, I know."

"Just hang in there, Eve. We'll leave this crazy life behind in a month."

"Really?"

"Yes, the light at the end of the tunnel is coming."

Eve hugged Wriley and felt assured.

*****

A few days later, Wriley was quietly discussing with Dean at the dining table while Eve was reading on the sofa.

"Does sis know yet?" Dean asked.

"No, I haven't told her," Wriley said as he looked at Eve, who glanced at him before continuing reading.

"Will she agree?" Dean asked.

"I don't know, but we have no choice. She will understand."

"That's such a risky move. Are you sure there is no other way?"

"I have thought it through. This is the best we can do."

After Wriley told Eve their escape plan, Eve walked up to the bedroom window and looked outside. Wriley walked over and hugged her from behind.

"Since I left the church with you, waves and waves of problems kept arising in our lives. I wonder if this is a sign that we are not meant to be together."

Wriley turned her around and grabbed her arms. "No, Eve, don't say that. I'm sorry that my life took a wrong turn, and I haven't been able to offer you the life you wanted. If my adopted parents were still alive, we would all be living together happily right now. Unfortunately, things turned out differently, and it led me down the path I am on today, but no matter where it takes me, I know one thing for sure: I am to be with you."

"Must we go through with this plan?"

"That is the only way we can break away."

"What if you don't make it?"

"Dean will take care of you."

Eve shook her head and cried. "That's not what I want. I gave up church to be with you, not anyone else."

Wriley grabbed her face. "I'll make it. I know how to get myself out. We'll be together, I promise," Wriley said and kissed her.

"Could I see Mother Mary and say my goodbyes to her?" Eve asked as they lay in bed.

"I'm sorry, Eve, but I can't risk anyone discovering our plans."

"I understand."

"How about once we move away, you can call her?"

"Okay."

*****

Wriley contacted his detective friend, requesting an audience with the Chief of the Police Department. The three met in secret.

"Chief, this is–" Detective Hugo was about to introduce.

"I know who he is. Eli De León, or should I say Wriley Corva. The boy shot and killed a man at the tender age of thirteen without any remorse. Yet you were found not guilty because Javier's lawyer insisted that it was an act of self-defense," Chief Darren said.

"He robbed and killed my adoptive parents," Wriley reminded.

"You should have let the law deal with him instead of taking the matter into your own hands. You were barely a teenager at that time. You have no business holding a gun, let alone killing someone," said Chief Darren.

"The law can't keep up with all these criminals running rampage around the state and country," said Wriley.

"So, you think you are a hero, like the Batman?"

"I never said I was. I just want to make those guys answer for their actions."

"How do I know if I can trust you?" Chief Darren asked.

"I've known Eli for years. He is a man of his word. He saved me once when I was pursuing one of Seth's men. He has helped us clean up a lot of messes. You can trust him," Detective Hugo vouched.

"What is in it for us this time?" Chief Darren asked.

"I'll help you exterminate your town of the ugliest pest, Seth Marsh, and his entourage. The biggest drug distributor in New York."

"We have been trying to get him for years," Detective Hugo commented.

"What about Javier?" Chief Darren asked.

"You don't have to worry about a man like Javier. His business is clean. Yes, he occasionally kills people, but you wouldn't want those guys in your city anyway. Trust me; no one will miss them," Wriley explained.

"And what do you want out of this?" Chief Darren asked.

"I want you to shoot me in the chest," said Wriley.

"You want us to kill you?" Chief Darren was confused.

"No, I want it to look like you kill me in front of everyone. So, I can walk away from all of this?"

"We will provide him with a safety vest," Detective Hugo added.

"You could've walked away all these times. Why now?" Chief Darren asked.

"This was only a temporary thing for me. I wanted to save enough for a better life. I was never in it for the long run," Wriley explained.

"You're Javier's adopted son. You think he will just let you walk?" Chief Darren asked.

"He can't keep a dead man by his side," replied Wriley.

*****

A couple of weeks later, Dean and Wriley dropped Eve off at the train station. Eve started to cry as she got out of the car.

Wriley wiped her tears and hugged her. "I'll be back shortly."

Eve nodded her head, trying hard to believe him.

"Go inside and be careful," Wriley instructed.

Eve took one last look at him before heading inside.

Dean pulled his car up to the destination.

Wriley turned to him. "No matter what, do not go inside. If I don't make it out in thirty minutes, just leave."

"Bro, I can't just leave you."

"You must."

"How am I supposed to answer to sis?"

"Do your best. If I don't make it, take care of her for me."

"Let's just call it off."

"No, we can't."

"Let me go instead of you, and you can just leave with Eve now."

"I can't let you sacrifice for me."

"You know I don't mind."

"I know, but I'm also Javier's son. I have to be by his side. I'll tell them that you're not feeling well, and they will believe me, but that excuse won't work for me. Besides, the cops only recognized me. If we change at the last minute, it will screw them up. Just promise me you will take good care of Eve."

"Yes, I promise I'll protect her with my life."

"And you will leave on time."

"Fine."

Wriley grabbed his shoulder. "You're a good brother. I'm glad we met."

"Same here. Be careful, Bro."

"I will," Wriley said as he got out of the car.

*****

Seth used the excuse of calling a truce to get rid of Javier and Wriley. Since Javier and Wriley knew ahead of time, they played along while buying out some of Seth's men. Wriley had already secretly alerted the police. When the police arrive, Wriley points his pistol at them, giving them a reason to shoot him in the chest, where he is protected with the bulletproof vest to fake his death.

"Javier." Seth walked up to hug him.

"Seth. Good to see you," Javier greeted.

The two men sat down.

"Look, I know what my men did to Eli's girl, and Eli already killed them. All of them. They are my closest and best men. I could make a big deal about it, but I won't. I just want some compensation for them and my bar, and we will call it even," Seth said.

"Oh, that simple?" Javier asked.

"Yes."

"What kind of compensation?"

"Ten million."

"Haha," Javier laughed, and his men did as well, except for Wriley. "What do you think, Eli?"

"I can kill him, and we will call it even," Wriley suggested.

Seth looked at Wriley. "I'll have to say, Javier, you didn't raise a son. You raised a monster."

Wriley gave him a look that could kill.

Javier looked at Wriley and smiled. "Forgive, my son. He is still not over the matter about his girl. However, I don't think your men and bar are worth ten mils."

"The business we do there is worth that much."

"I see. What about one?"

"No."

"No? What if I don't agree to your deal?"

"You won't be able to walk out of here."

Javier looked around, acting as if he was scared. "That confident?"

Seth smirked and handed him the tablet. "Make the transfer, or the bomb under your seat will go off. If you stand up, it will also explode."

"Well, then, let's test it out," Javier said as he rose slowly.

"No, don't," Seth said as he and his men hurried to hide behind the couch.

After anticipating the explosion, there was only silence, and Javier and his men started laughing.

"You tried to scare me with this silly trick?" Javier grabbed the bomb from Diro's hand and threw it over to them.

Seth and his men stood up, looking confused. "What happened to the bomb?" Seth asked one of his men, who shrugged, clueless as he was.

"Now, do you still want that ten million?" Javier asked.

"One is fine," Seth said with a smile as he straightened his suit.

"How about nada?" Javier said.

Suddenly, most of the guns in the room pointed at Seth and his few loyal men, who also drew out their weapons to defend themselves.

Seth knew he had lost to Javier. "Look," Seth started, but Wriley didn't give him a chance to speak as he fired right into his forehead.

Javier's men started firing at the rest of Seth's men.

Then the cops showed up. As soon as Javier saw the cops, he grabbed the gun from Ben's hand and started firing at Wriley. One bullet into Wriley's left waist and the other on his right thigh. Wriley dropped to the ground.

"How dare you betray us, working for the cops," Javier shouted.

"Freeze!" The cops called out.

"Drop your weapons," Detective Hugo commanded.

Javier happily dropped his gun and raised his hands in a peaceful surrender.

Detective Hugo rushed over to Wriley's side. "Eli," he called out, but Wriley was unconscious.

*****

At twenty-nine minutes, Dean was getting anxious as there was no sign of Wriley. Then, the thirty-minute mark came up. Dean was debating whether to drive off. He knew he made a promise to Wriley, but at the same time, he couldn't bear to step on the gas. He decided to wait a minute longer. Still, no sign, so another minute, then another. Each minute seems like a decade. After an additional ten minutes, Dean shook his head and drove away.

"Goodbye, Bro," Dean said regrettably.

*****

Eve has been waiting anxiously at the train station. She stood up when she spotted Dean from afar. As Dean approached her, Eve's eyes searched for Wriley but saw no sign of him. Then she looked straight at Dean, who sadly shook his head. Eve dropped the bag of clothes on the ground. Her worst nightmare came true. Dean reached down to grab the bag.

"We have to go," Dean said.

Eve couldn't move.

"Sis, we got to go now."

Eve quietly followed Dean.

They settled down in a private suite on the train. Eve started to cry as soon as she sat down.

"I'm sorry, sis. I can't bring him back to you," Dean said as he shed tears himself.

Eve couldn't say or do anything other than cry. She couldn't blame Dean nor Wriley or anyone else but herself. God was definitely making her pay for renouncing her vows, she thought. Eve looked outside the window while touching her belly. Dean noticed her gesture.

"Does he know?" Dean asked.

Eve shook her head.

Dean closed his eyes and let out a deep sigh before leaning back. He wondered if Wriley would have changed the plan if he found out Eve was pregnant, but that question would never be answered.

*****

"Eve, you not only took my Eli away but also made me lose everything. I will not let you live in peace. You have to pay for this," Megan said inside her room.

Javier and his men have been arrested, but Javier knew he would get out in no time with the money he got.

Chapter 16
Brother

Dean and Eve settled down in a small town in Washington as Wriley had instructed. Eve continued to mourn the loss of Wriley for the next few days behind closed door. She grieved for not being able to see him one last time. Grieved for their ill-fated love. She prayed to God to forgive all of Wriley's sins and accept him into God's kingdom.

Dean knocked on Eve's door, who was weeping in bed. "Sis, please come have dinner."

"I'm not hungry."

"I know you don't feel like eating, but you have to think about the baby, and Bro wouldn't want you to be like this."

Eve had forgotten about the baby, the only remnant of Wriley. She will do whatever it takes to protect their baby. Eve touched her belly, then sat up and wiped her tears. A little later, she opened the door to face Dean.

"Thank you, Dean."

Dean smiled at her.

"Maybe I should contact Mother Mary. Perhaps she will let me stay at the church for a while until I find my own place," Eve said while they were eating.

"No, sis, you can't go back to New York, especially to the church. It may affect everyone there. I can't risk others finding out about you, and if they know that you're carrying Bro's baby, they will not let you live in peace."

Eve was terrified at the thought of potential harm to her baby. "I guess I will stay here then."

"Yes, stick with me. I'll do whatever it takes to make sure you and the baby are safe."

"I appreciate you watching over us, but I don't want to trouble you."

"It's no trouble. I made a promise to Bro."

"I know you're doing it because Wriley requested, but I don't want you to have to take responsibility for someone else."

"I really don't mind. It's my pleasure to care for the two most valuable things to Bro, you and the baby. You're like my family as well. I know you're probably not comfortable living with me, but just think of me as your brother. I wish I could trade my life for his, but I can't."

"Wriley is very blessed to have a loyal friend like you."

"I know he would have done the same for me."

A couple of days later, Dean contemplated the best way to protect Eve and her unborn child.

"Sis, I think we should move to Iceland," Dean said as they sat on the couch.

"Why Iceland?"

"Just in case the bad guys traced us here. I want to take you out of the country where you can safely give birth. Iceland is a pretty peaceful and safe country. No one would find us there."

"I'll do what you think is best."

"Okay, I'll book the tickets."

*****

They arrived in a quiet town in Iceland.

"We'll stay here for the time being until I find a better place," Dean said as they looked around the apartment.

"This is fine. Once we settle down, I should look for a job."

"Bro left you a lot of money to make sure you can live a comfortable life without having to work."

"I know, but I don't want to stay at home all day. I should step out and see the world a little."

"If you're bored, I'll get you books to read, puzzles to do, or whatever else you're interested in."

"I can't sit at home and read books for the rest of my life."

"That's true. I know what you mean. I've been pretty bored sitting at home doing nothing. Before, when I was working with Bro, I couldn't wait to have some downtime. Now, I wish I could work beside him again. Because you're pregnant now, I think you should stay home for the time being, and after you have the baby, you can look for a job. Is that okay?"

Eve nodded.

"We can go for a walk every day, so you're not always cooped up inside."

"Okay."

"And if you ever need money for anything, just let me know."

"Could I keep some money in case I need to buy any personal stuff?"

“Sure.” Dean walked over to a draw and pull out a pack of cash. “Here is a thousand. Let me know if you need more.” Dean handed her the money.

“I won’t need that much. A hundred should be enough.”

“Just keep it. You never know when you may need it.”

“Okay. Thank you, Dean.”

“Don’t thank me. These are Bro’s money, and they are yours now. I’m just helping you manage it.”

*****

Eve walked out of her room. “Dean, could you take me to the hospital? I think I’m going into labor.”

Dean quickly jumped off the couch. “Yes!”

Dean carried her into the hospital. “Help, please! She is going into labor!”

A staff member rushed over. “Here, put her in the wheelchair.”

Dean sat her down, and the staff pushed her to a room. Dean followed them but stood outside. A couple of minutes later, more staff came by to help deliver the baby.

“Are you the husband? Would you like to come inside?” A nurse asked.

“No, I’m not her husband. I’m her brother-in-law,” Dean replied.

“Oh, where is her husband?”

“He is not here right now.”

“I see. Okay, we’ll tell you when you can come in.”

“Thank you.”

Eve wished Wriley could be right beside her during the painful delivery to hold her hand. Fortunately, the birthing was smooth without any complications.

Dean anxiously watched the staff exit the room. "Dean, you can come inside and see your nephew now," the female doctor said.

Dean smiled brightly. "Thank you."

"Hello, sis."

"Hi, Dean. Would you like to hold him?"

"Yes, may I?"

"Of course." Eve carefully handed him the baby.

"Hello, little man. I can see Bro in him. If Bro were here, he would have been such a proud father."

Eve smiled but cried on the inside. She felt sorry for her son not having a chance to know his father just like how she never got to know hers. She also can't imagine how happy Wriley would have been to hold their son in his arms. It was almost like the pictures he painted. The only thing missing was the painter.

"Are you planning to marry and have children of your own?" Eve asked Dean to distract her own mind.

"I would love to someday."

"Thank you for taking care of us all this time."

"It's my honor that Bro entrusted you two to me."

"Would you like to be his godfather?"

"I would love to."

"You can get a job now and don't have to worry about staying home to take care of me."

"Now that there is this little guy, I might stay home and hang out with him for a while before I start work."

Eve smiled at them.

"Actually, I think we should move to another town. They have your name in the system now. It's better to move somewhere else," Dean suggested.

"Okay."

"Have you thought of a name for him?" Dean asked.

"Let's call him Ley. It's the last three letters of Wriley's name," said Eve.

"Ley. I like it."

*****

They moved to a new town for a year.

The doorbell rang, and Eve answered.

"Hi, Eve. Hello, Ley," Zelda greeted. She was their neighbor.

"Hello, Zelda," Eve greeted back.

"Is Dean home?"

"Yes, he is getting ready for work. You want to talk to him."

Dean was working as a chef at a local restaurant.

"Oh, it's not necessary."

"That's all right. Let me call him."

"Okay."

"Dean, Zelda is here to see you."

"Okay." Dean walked out. "Hello," Dean greeted.

"Hi, Dean. I prepared this meatloaf for you guys."

Dean grabbed the container. "Why, thank you, that's kind of you."

"It's nothing much. I just happened to make extra."

"Thank you, Zelda," Eve said.

"You're welcome. Well, enjoy your lunch."

"Thanks. Bye," Dean said.

"Bye-bye," Zelda said.

"Zelda is a sweet girl, and I think she really likes you. Have you thought of going out with her?" Eve asked as she watched Dean set up the food on the table.

"I just started working again. I want to make sure our lives are stable before I bring someone else into them."

"Dean, if it's because of me—"

"No, sis. It's not you. Zelda may be a nice girl, but I'm not ready at this time."

"I see."

"Let's eat."

"Okay." Eve settled Ley down in his high chair and sat down.

Dean couldn't tell Eve that he had fallen for her and wanted to marry her.

"Have you thought of remarrying?" Dean asked.

Eve shook her head. "No."

"Eve."

"Hmm?"

"Since we live together, and I can never leave you. I was wondering—" Dean hesitated with his words.

"Wonder what?"

"Oh, uhm, I was wondering if we should buy a house and settle down for good."

"Sure, that's fine."

"I've been doing some research and found an ideal place for us to live out the rest of our days."

"You want to move again?"

"Yes."

"What about Zelda?"

Dean shook his head. "I don't think it's going to happen."

"Do you not like her?"

"I just never thought about it."

"Dean."

"I'm too focused on my career right now."

"Okay. We will do as you suggest."

Dean smiled at her. He wanted so badly to confess, even though he knew in her heart there was only Wriley. It was also out of respect for his Bro that he couldn't bring himself to say the words.

Chapter 17
Game

Over a year later, in a small town in Iceland. A group of kids exited the church after a Bible lesson, while Eve stayed behind to put the Bibles away. On her way out, her eyes gaze up at a man heading toward the church. She stopped in her footsteps at the top of the stairs after she saw his face. The man also paused and looked up at her. Eve couldn't believe her eyes and wondered if this was a dream, or if somehow in the world, there was another man who looked exactly like Wriley.

"Eve."

Eve started to cry at the sound of him calling her name. Then suddenly, a voice of child called out from behind Wriley.

"Mommy."

Wriley immediately turned around to see Dean carrying a little boy. Dean was also shocked to see Wriley.

"Bro, you're alive!"

Wriley looked at the child and back at Eve. Eve still didn't say anything, so Wriley turned to Dean. Dean figured Wriley must be curious about Ley, so he set Ley down on the ground.

"Look, Ley. There is your father. Go to your daddy." Dean nudged Ley.

Wriley heart melted at the news that he has a son. He crouched to receive Ley, who was stumbling over to him. He looked at Ley and touched his face.

"My son," Wriley said softly.

"Daddy?" Ley called out. He has his father's eyes and brows.

Wriley nodded with a smile and hugged him. "Yes, yes." Wriley held him tightly.

Eve was still too emotional to move while Dean was smiling happily at this beautiful reunion. Wriley picked Ley up and looked at Eve.

"What happened that day?" Dean asked Wriley over dinner.

"Javier shot me," replied Wriley.

"What?"

"He was trying to help me."

"I don't get it."

"He figured that I wanted to leave with Eve and confronted me, so I had to admit the whole thing to him."

*****

Flashback to three years ago. Javier received word that Wriley had dismissed all the guards and dropped Eve off at the train station. Before they met with Seth, Javier pulled Wriley to the side and had a chat with him in the hallway.

"Are you planning to elope with Eve?" Javier asked.

"Yes."

"You're going to leave all this behind, including me?"

"Yes."

"I love you like a son, but it seems like you never fully trust me."

"Did you trust me? I know you have men watching me."

"Not all the time. I did it to protect you."

"What I did was to protect myself as well."

"You know, I was hoping you could take over for me one day. Even though Megan is my daughter, she is a woman. She won't know how to run this business."

"I know, but before I met you, I already made a promise to Eve. A promise I cannot break. Especially with everything that she went through. I owe it to her."

"Why didn't you tell me that that is your goal?"

"I was afraid that you might not agree to let us go, then it may be harder to leave."

Javier looked away and sighed. "Yes, I would hate to see you go, but I could also understand. I already told you I could help arrange a safe and peaceful life for you both and eventually probably let you go for good. All you have to do is talk to me."

"I'm sorry, for Eve's sake, I didn't dare to risk our only chance."

Javier stared at Wriley.

When the cops showed up, Javier didn't want Wriley to be implicated, so he shot Wriley to make it seem like Wriley was innocent. He did make sure that it won't kill Wriley either. Wriley remained in the hospital for one week. After that, he waited a month for his wounds to heal and things to calm down before finding Eve and Dean. Javier went to prison and got out less than a year later due to his good lawyers.

*****

Wriley went to the town in Washington as he instructed Dean to take Eve. Knocking on the door of the apartment that he had rented for them, he anxiously waited to see Eve again, but to his surprise, a stranger answered. An elderly woman cautiously opened the door.

"Can I help you, Sir?" she asked.

Wriley was taken aback a bit before asking, "Hi, I'm looking for Eve or Dean."

"Sorry, there is no one here by that name."

"How long have you lived here?" Wriley asked.

"Over a week ago."

"I see, they must have moved then. Thank you, and sorry to bother you."

"No problem." The woman closed the door.

Wriley called Dean, but the response he got was. "This number is no longer in service."

Wriley went to the office of the apartment and checked with the staff.

"Hi, how can I help you?" A lady in her mid-forties asked.

"Hi, I wanted to ask about the previous tenant in apartment #7, Dean or Eve. I guess they are not there anymore."

"And what is your relation to them?"

"Eve is my wife, and Dean is my brother. I actually rented the apartment for us and told them to settle in first. I just returned from a business trip and can't seem to find them anymore. Can't get a hold of them over the phone either."

"Oh, ok let me check." The lady looked up the contract on the computer. "It looks like they only stayed here for a couple of days and left right after that."

"Did they say where they were moving to or leave any message?"

"I'm sorry, I have no idea. They didn't leave anything behind."

"I see, well, thank you for your help."

"You're welcome. Is there anything I can help you with?"

"No that's it. Thanks."

"You're welcome. Have a good day."

"You too." Wriley walked away with disappointment and frustration over Eve's whereabouts.

After spending months searching every corner of the state and asking folks about them, Wriley realized they were no longer there.

"Dean, where did you take her?" Wriley asked himself out loud while sitting in his car. He was also worried that something bad has happened to them but tried to brush the thought aside.

He racked his brain, thinking of places that Dean might have gone. Then suddenly, he recalled something.

A couple of weeks before they executed the plan, Wriley searched for a place to settle down, and Dean was nearby.

"Hey, Bro. I heard Iceland is the most peaceful country in the world," Dean shared.

"It's too far away," said Wriley.

"Isn't far good?"

"I want to be in the States."

"Just saying."

"Iceland," Wriley said aloud, and was on the next plane to Iceland. He has been searching every town since.

*****

Back to the present.

"Why didn't you stick with the plan?" Wriley asked Dean.

"I initially did. We stayed there for a couple of days, but then, since Eve was pregnant, I didn't want to risk us being discovered. I wanted to make sure she and the child are safe, so I decided to take them here. I ditched the phone because I didn't want anyone to trace us. We have move twice since we came to Iceland, once after she gave birth and then a year later, before I found this perfect town to settle in." Dean explained.

"I see."

"Sorry for making you search for us. I thought you were dead. Otherwise, I would have left some clues for you. But everything I did was to protect Eve and your child."

"I understand. It's all right. It's in the past now. Thank you for taking care of them all these years," Wriley said.

"So did Javier know that you were the one who contacted the cops?" Dean was curious.

"I don't think so, I never confess to him about that part."

"I see, probably that's for the better," Dean commented.

Eve ate her dinner in silence while listening to their conversations without adding to them. She kept her eyes on her food and never gazed up once at them.

Wriley noticed Eve had been quiet all evening. He couldn't imagine what she was thinking. She should be happy to see him, yet her face tells a different tale.

Dean helped Eve clean up after dinner while Wriley spent time with Ley.

Wriley watched Eve put Ley to bed, then followed her quietly back to her room. Wriley closed the door behind him and walked up to Eve, who had her back toward him. Wriley slowly wrapped his arms around her from the back. Eve forgot what it felt like to be in his embrace. She closed her eyes to take it in for a moment, then started to shake her head and broke away.

"I can't do this again," Eve said as she turned around to face him.

"Eve."

"Every time we are together, terrible things happen. I thought you were dead. I cope with it, accept my fate, and move on. You can't just suddenly show up like this and expect everything to go back to normal again."

"Eve, I know."

"You don't know. You don't know how many tears I shed each night from missing you. How painful it is to know that Ley will grow up without meeting his father. I was hoping our child would have a better life than us, where he lived with both his mother and father. Nor do you know how fearful I am that God won't stop punishing me, that he may take Ley from me at any instant. So please, don't come back into my life. I already made peace with being without you. I won't be able to handle it anymore if something else happens."

Wriley heart was drenched with her tears as he wiped her face. "Eve, I know there is nothing I can do to make up for all the pain and suffering you had to endure all these years. I don't deserve your forgiveness either for dragging you from heaven to hell. But Eve, I have been searching for you tirelessly, nonstop, for the past few years to fulfill the promise I made to you. Now that I have found you, how can you expect me to let you go?"

"I forgive you, and I won't hold you to your promise so you can move on. Find another woman who is better than me."

Wriley shook his head and grabbed her arms. "No, there is no other woman in this world who is better than you. Besides, we have a child now. Don't you want him to grow up with both of his parents? Can you bear for him to lose his father after we just reunited?"

Eve looked downward, knowing what he said made sense. "But if something were to happen to you again, it wouldn't be fair to him to deal with such loss."

"Nothing will happen to me. I'm here now, safe and sound in front of you as promised. We can truly be together from now on. My worst fear is that Javier won't let us go, but it turns out he is supportive of us. Javier's worst enemy has also been eliminated. No one will bother us anymore. We can live peacefully as a family from now on."

Eve remained silent as she looked at Wriley. She didn't want to continue to fall for false hope again. "You always paint these beautiful pictures of our lives together, and I fall for them every single time, only to be disappointed over and over again."

"We have fought so hard to be together, Eve, don't give up on us now. I never gave up on you and never will. I will hold on to you until the end of time," Wriley wrapped his arms around Eve.

Once again, like a gullible person, Eve gave in to Wriley's promises as she raised her arms to hug him. Wriley started to kiss her shoulder, then her neck, cheek, and finally her mouth. He scooped her up and carried her over to the bed. The two made love like it was the last night on earth.

"How was it like living with Dean for the past few years?" Wriley asked as he stroked her hair with half of Eve's body lying on top of his chest.

"Dean has done a lot for us. He has taken good care of Ley and me."

"That's good. He is the only person in this world I could trust."

"I feel bad sometimes because I didn't want to be his burden. He could have been living his own life instead of always worrying about us."

"Don't worry, I'm sure he doesn't mind. Dean is the kind of person who will never break his promises."

"I know, which makes me feel more uncomfortable. Like he has to shoulder something he shouldn't have to."

"I'll talk to him tomorrow. Now that I'm here, he can go live his own life."

"Yes. I think we have troubled him enough. He should find a girl and settle down. In the last town we stayed, there was a lovely neighbor who liked him, but I guess Dean didn't feel the same about her."

"I didn't know he was that picky."

"I think he just wanted to focus on ensuring our safety."

"Probably. Now that we are united as a family, we can finally live out the life we have always dreamt of. You, me, Ley, and his uncle Dean. We can have a couple more kids as well."

Eve recalled the day she gave birth to Ley without Wriley by her side. "It was painful giving birth to Ley. How I wish you were there with me, but you weren't."

Wriley kissed her head and rubbed her back. "I'm sorry I wasn't there with you for the birth of Ley, but I promise I will be right next to you for future births. That is, if you want to have more kids. We don't have to."

After a moment of silence, Eve spoke up. "Would you like to have another son or daughter?"

"I would like to have a girl. It would be wonderful if she could look like you. Little Eve would be adorable." Wriley smiled. "But I'm okay with another boy as well. What about you?"

"I'll take whatever God gives us."

"Our family will never be apart again."

"Umm." Eve nodded.

After getting dressed, Wriley walked over to Eve, still sleeping in bed. He placed a hand on her head and kissed her forehead before walking outside.

Eve woke a little later and found Wriley missing. She threw on a bathrobe and rushed out to make sure yesterday wasn't a dream.

"Wriley!" Eve called out.

"Yes?" Wriley answered from the kitchen.

Eve breathed out a sigh of relief when she saw his face. He looked at her as she walked over and hugged him from the back; Wriley was cooking.

"I'm afraid that it was all a dream. I wanted to make sure you're still here."

Wriley put down the spatula and turned around. He cupped her face with his hands. "You're not dreaming, and I'm not going anywhere," Wriley smiled warmly and gave her a peck on the lips. "Go get dressed. Breakfast is almost ready."

Eve nodded and walked away as Wriley grinned to himself.

Wriley prepared breakfast for them, and they all enjoyed eating together as a happy family. Eve started to have hope and could see a happy ending for them.

"Thanks, Dean, for taking care of Eve and Ley all these years. I owe you big time," said Wriley.

Dean smiled shyly. "It's nothing, Bro. I owe you much more. Besides, it's nice to retire from that work and live in this peaceful town. Plus, I get to play with this little guy," Dean tickled Ley and made him laugh.

Both Eve and Wriley smiled at them.

"You haven't found a girl yet?" Wriley asked.

"Nope, still looking."

"That's because he has been busy taking care of us," Eve commented, appreciating Dean's help all these times.

"No, I just haven't met the right one yet," Dean lied so that they wouldn't feel bad as he sneaked a glance at Eve.

Wriley watched Dean and caught on fast. "I'm here now, so you are free to travel around."

"Yeah, I will. I might try opening a restaurant."

"You should. You're a good cook," Eve supported.

"Yes, do it. I'll support you. You can take my money," Wriley offered.

"That won't be necessary. I also have my own savings from all these years."

"That's fine as well. You know you can always go to me for help."

"I know. Thanks, Bro."

After breakfast, Dean and Wriley had a chat in the backyard.

"It's so good seeing you again, Bro," said Dean.

"It's good seeing you as well. Are you planning to move back to the States?" Wriley asked.

Dean shook his head. "No. I like living here."

"Are you going to stick around town then or move somewhere else?" Wriley asked.

"I'm not sure yet. I'll miss playing with Ley and hanging with you guys. Especially since we haven't seen each other for the past few years."

"I'm sure Eve and Ley would also miss you if you move away."

"I'll miss them for sure, but now that they have you, they may forget me after a while."

"No, they won't. You're a huge part of their lives."

Dean smiled.

"Dean?" Wriley asked.

"Yeah?"

"Do you like Eve?"

Dean stared at him. "Bro, I—"

"You don't have to hide from me."

Dean was silent for a moment. "I'm sorry. After living with Eve for a while, I didn't know when, but I started developing feelings for her. But I know she is your woman, and I could never betray you. Besides, she only has you in her heart."

Wriley grabbed Dean's shoulder. "You don't have to apologize to me. Any man who is around Eve long enough would fall for her. What is not to love about Eve? I don't blame you, so don't feel bad. I'm sure it must have been hard on you."

"In her eyes, I can never replace you. No one can."

"Dean, I'm sorry that the woman you want to be with can't reciprocate the same feelings. The love between Eve and me is rooted too deep for anything to come in between. But I'm sure you will find a wonderful woman that you can share this special bond with one of these days. I know you will be a great husband to that lucky girl."

Dean touched his hand. "Thank you, Bro."

"No, thank you, brother." Wriley hugged him.

"What if I were with Eve? What would you do?" Dean was curious.

"I can understand, but I'll have to get her back. You know I can never let her go."

Dean smiled. "I know."

"Even if I have to crawl out of hell, I'll be with her."

"I believe you."

In the evening, they were hanging out in the living room playing with Ley when the doorbell rang.

"I'll get it." Eve stood up and walked over to the door.

Eve opened it, and suddenly a gunshot went off at the same time as Eve saw Megan's face.

"Eve!" Wriley called out as he and Dean rushed over.

Eve fell back into Wriley's arms as Dean drew out a gun from his back and shot Megan in the chest and head. She dropped to the ground.

Megan, without her dad's knowledge and consent, has hired a fellow to secretly follow Wriley's every move from the moment he was discharged from the hospital. She hated Eve to the core, and the thirst for revenge has made the worst of her. Megan cannot allow Eve to live happily ever after with Wriley, even at the cost of her own life.

Ley was scared by the loud noise and cried. Dean went over to comfort him.

"Eve, Eve," Wriley called her name with his hand over her chest, trying to stop the bleeding.

Eve tried to catch her breath before speaking. "Please take care of Ley, don't let him know about your past."

"I'll take good care of him. Eve, you'll be fine. Let me take you to the hospital."

Eve shook her head and touched Wriley's face. "It's either you or me. I'd rather it's me."

"No, Eve. If I had known my presence would lead to this, I would have stayed far away."

Eve shook her head as tears poured out of her eyes. "I never regret it, never. I got to be with the man I love, however brief it was, and gave birth to a beautiful child. I experienced the life of a wife and a mother; that's plenty for me," she knew very well that this was the end, just as she had dread. It seems like God must not want them to be together.

"Eve, don't say anything. Everything is going to be okay," Wriley said, but they both knew those words were to comfort him, not her.

"Promise me you won't blame him. Don't hate God. I'll wait for you. I'll make sure he opens the gate when you come." Those were Eve's last words before her hand dropped to her side.

"Eve! No! Eve! Please don't leave me. I only live for you," Wriley cried out as he clenched her body. Then he let out a scream that frightened Ley. "Why? God, why?" If he had the power, he would destroy heaven and earth in that instant for separating Eve and him forever.

Dean picked Ley up and walked over to them.

"Mommy?" Ley reached out his hand to her, too young to understand. Perhaps that was for the best.

Dean also cried. He had put in so much effort to keep Eve safe for the past three years, and now it was all in vain.

Wriley carried Eve's lifeless body into the church, and Dean followed him with Ley in his arms. Wriley stood facing the cross.

"This is what you wanted? You won't stop until one of us is dead. Are you satisfied?"

"Bro, please. Let Eve rest in peace. It will break her heart to see you like this."

Wriley buried Eve in the church's graveyard with a private service from the priest. She finally gets to return to the church. That was probably the only place she felt most safe.

Wriley stood quietly in front of her grave with Dean and Ley. He wondered if his selfish need to be with her had cost Eve her life and whether it was a mistake to take her away from the church in the first place. She could still be living a peaceful life there.

Dean started to recall all the beautiful memories he shared with Eve and Ley. He couldn't believe that just like that, she was gone. In a moment of rage, Dean turned and grabbed Wriley's shirt. "Bro, I love you, but—" Dean choked up. "I really want to punch you right now." Dean held up his fist.

"Do it," Wriley encouraged.

Dean hesitated and shook his head. "But I know Eve will be sad if I hurt you." Dean started to cry. "I fell in love with Eve the day she had to give birth alone without her husband, and all I could do was stand and wait in the hallway because I don't have the right to be by her side."

"You know I would be there if I could."

"I know, but you weren't. You were not there when she needed you the most. When she gave birth to your son. And I have kept my promise to you and watched over her for the past three years. You showed up for only one day, and now Eve is gone. After a year, she finally stopped crying and lived a peaceful life with her son, but your selfish desire to be with her has cost Eve her life and Ley's his mother. I also love Eve, but I don't have to have her. Your love is toxic. It has destroyed her hopes and dreams. She is lying under there because of you. She is gone, Bro, gone!" Dean sobbed as he leaned his head on Wriley's shoulder.

Wriley brought up his hand and placed it on Dean's neck, hugging him tightly. "You're right. Everything you said is right. Eve is dead because of me, because I can't stand losing her. Because I couldn't let her go."

"And what I hate the most is that she never once blamed you. Never did, but someone has to."

Wriley stroked his head. "You're right to blame me."

Wriley lay awake most of that night holding Ley. When he finally fell asleep, he dreamt that he returned to the church after his adopted parents died. There, he grew up with Eve, and when they came of age, they left the church together hand-in-hand, ready to take on the world together with a smile. Unfortunately, Wriley woke to a solemn reality. One without Eve.

Wriley walked into the church and sat down on the pew, staring at Christ on the cross. "You greedy old man. You have so many angels around you. Why must you take Eve away from me, from us? Is it because I killed your other sons? But it's not my fault. You're the one who threw me into that kind of life when you took my parents away. You were against me from the very beginning. Why? All I wanted was a family. Why can't you give us a moment of peace? Is this a game to you? What have we done to deserve this? What has she done wrong?" Wriley jumped up and argued in vain with the cross. "Answer my fucking questions! I know you can hear me!"

There was only silence as his voice echoed in the tiny church.

"I know Eve doesn't want me to hate you, but I can't. I will never forgive you. I didn't fail her. You failed her," Wriley said before walking out.

Dean was waiting with Ley outside. Wriley bent down to pick Ley up and kissed his cheek. Wriley was glad Ley had his mother's smile, something he could hold on to.

The three of them walked away from the church, never to look back again.

Alternative Ending

Wriley carried Eve's lifeless body into the church, and Dean followed with Ley in his arms. Wriley stood facing the cross.

"This is what you wanted? You won't stop until one of us is dead. Are you satisfied?" Wriley gently laid Eve down on the floor and sat down with his arms hanging off his arched knees. "Here is your chance to prove me wrong, save her."

"Bro, you shouldn't be like this," said Dean.

"Leave me!" Wriley shouted.

"Mommy," Ley called out in fear.

"Take Ley out of here," Wriley instructed.

Dean sighed before walking out with Ley.

"Eve, do you still remember the scent of gardenia? Whenever I think of you, I suddenly smell the fragrance around me. I was planning to grow you a garden of gardenias. Eve, talk to me. I am nothing without you. Incomplete without you. You're the closest thing to heaven. How am I supposed to move on by myself? God, show me that you're merciful. Give us a chance."

After a long silence, Eve suddenly gasped softly for air.

"Eve!" Wriley cried out.

About the Author

QC Ngo was born in Vietnam. At two years old, she and her family fled to Thailand. There, they lived in the refugee camps for over three years before residing in San Diego. She majored in human biology during her undergraduate years at UCSD and received her Doctor of Pharmacy degree in Utah. She worked for six years for the veteran health care system in Tennessee and California before secretly pursuing her passion for writing. Most of her fictions were inspired by real people and events.

Blurb

When a mafia member falls in love with a nun, can they truly be together? Eve and Wriley grew up in the church orphanage. Wriley was later adopted and promised to come back for her in a year, but he couldn't make it due to unfortunate life circumstances. When Wriley showed up twelve years later, Eve was now a nun. The road to being together was full of thorns. With their undying love for each other, can they overcome all the obstacles and live out a fairy tale ending?

Made in the USA
Coppell, TX
15 April 2026

75744217R00114